Killer Island

FRANCIS LECANE

authorHOUSE®

AuthorHouse™ UK Ltd.
500 Avebury Boulevard
Central Milton Keynes, MK9 2BE
www.authorhouse.co.uk
Phone: 08001974150

Published by AuthorHouse 1/16/2012

ISBN: 978-1-4678-7828-9 (sc)
ISBN: 978-1-4678-7829-6 (e)

KILLER ISLAND

Chapter One

When I first cast eyes on that island all those months ago little did I realise what extreme pleasure and pain it would bring into my life. I was totally unprepared for the life changing, not to say job changing, aspects of it and how it has altered me and my approach to life generally.

Gruinard Island of ill repute, shunned by the mainland locals, shunned by wild life, only visited by extreme idiots with nothing better to do: I should have steered well clear of it. But then I'd never have met and fallen in love with Catriona, or her me; at least I hope it's love and not some ghastly form of Twenty-First Century lust!

The island, a tiny speck a mile or so from the North West mainland of Scotland, sits alone like a leper in the crystal sea. Contaminated by government order, way back before I was born, but still a major biohazard. No creatures live there. The very occasional rabbit, but they don't breed. No insects, no skinks, no voles or mice. Nada. Nothing. Zilch. Not quite true, I hear you say; two white tailed fish eagles have been seen flying over and maybe breeding on the island. There are living creatures on the island, but not many, considering that the greatest predator of all, the human, hasn't been in residence or even left much of a mark in seventy years.

In 1942 the ministry of biological and chemical weapons, not known by that title then, sanctioned a destructive test on some captive sheep, to see if they would contract the deadly form of anthrax if they were blown up with bombs containing anthrax spores. Those guys! They must have realised the wee beasties would die from the effect of the high explosive let alone the spores. Nevertheless they imported a flock of sixty sheep onto the island, proceeded to pen them up in different parts and then exploded anthrax bombs over them. Surprise, surprise, they all died, some sooner than later, some later as their respiratory systems were compromised by the bacillus. Mind you, this was 1942 and subtlety was not high in the order of things. Later on after the remains of the sheep had been disposed of and things had settled down somewhat, one of the carcasses escaped, God knows how, and ended up on the mainland driven there by the vagaries of the weather. It contaminated several mainland sheep and other livestock, all of which had to be put down and the matter was hushed up. Luckily for the authorities nothing further transpired, but the island was a mess and it was declared out of bounds. Signs were put up, and the locals stopped visiting. But anthrax can live in the soil for hundreds if not thousands of years, lying dormant and just waiting to become active again. So in the Seventies the authorities decided in their half-hearted way to decontaminate the place. A team of operatives, dressed in those silly yellow plastic suits, landed on the island and proceeded to dig up the top soil and take it away. Then they laid pipe lines perforated along their length and pumped carbolic acid through them. In this way is science served. It had not the slightest effect, and the island remained contaminated. Back in London, the

Ministry washed its hands of the whole thing and declared the island safe! Still the locals refused to visit.

Now its 2011 - seventy years since nearly everyone who was connected has passed on to the great maker in the sky, or that composter and soil improver that the local council recyclers are so proud of. Even the mainland locals, braw lads and lassies of middle age shake their heads in a way and suck on what teeth they have left as they discuss the merits of taking me out to the island!

General opinion: no way. What does a callow youth from the city on a motorbike, a BMW what's more, want from the island? German motorbike indeed; what's wrong with a Triumph or a Kawasaki for that matter? Poof's bike, with its belt drive and its gleaming paintwork! Only fit for city gays and other non-entities!

'Anyway, Brucie, you notice he never offered anything to get taken out to the island. Fucking cheapskate. We'll leave him steep in his own shite.'

It turned out the only German within miles who might have a motorbike was an unwashed dope-head living on a croft he had bought with an inheritance from his father, whom it was alleged was a high ranking SS officer during the war. He was well enough thought of, the German, but his aversion to dentists had left him with tombstone teeth that oozed yellow pus and an odour that kept most people at bay. His only visitors were other dope smokers who, once they were so stoned on the strong skunk that the German grew, were only too inclined to breathe his breath as a reminder that they were still alive! He picked mussels for a living, but in the close season he had seen the fruits of his labours glowing green beneath the shallow seas off the island and he had been quite put off. Occasionally he would be seen blasting through the town on his 250cc Honda, with his wild grey hair blowing behind him and a miasma of mussels, dung and poor dental hygiene following after. I only mention him because he was one of the true eccentrics of this world. A poor deluded foreigner who thought it possible to make a living in the great wen let alone the Great Glen. His croft was a tumbledown home, what was left of the stone-walled former croft house he had renovated, and pulled his travelling truck up into the shelter of the lichen-covered stones. Being a pacifist at heart, he refused to kill an animal, so his veg and crops and precious dope were a beauty feast for the fat and fecund rabbits that really owned the land on which he strode.

I was now sitting in the bar of the Gruinard Bay Arms. A nicely renovated long house style pub with a car park and a monthly ceilidh from the likes of the Mcphearson Show band, or this month's attraction: Angus McFee and the Mussel Men. Mustn't miss them! A peat fire burnt in the fireplace, though it was high summer and the other clientele, who numbered about six to eight brawny wool jersied fishermen, all drinking pints of some ubiquitous continental lager.

The door to the bar swung open and an apparition came in. Not above five foot eight, with beautiful, long plaited red hair that hung down her back like a silken rope. Green eyes and under the over enveloping cagoule a body to die for, at least I hoped so!

'Yo Catriona!' yelled one of the braw lads. She nodded her greetings, 'Here's a laddie wants shifting out to the anthrax island; you got your boat?' She looked over in my direction. A piercing green gaze that left me jellified from the knees.

'Maybe. I've an inkling to see what it's like over there.' She pulled a bar stool away from the bar and perched up on it. I sidled over like a wet spaniel, its tongue hanging down for a good petting.

'Hi! I'm Davie.' What she saw puts most people off, but there are some who've called me handsome and defined it with, little shite! A twenty-five year old surf-haired youth, with a broken nose and a thin black beard that started up under one ear and ran down like oily rain all the way to the other ear. Teeth all my own and scrupulously looked after, so that when I smiled, which I tried to do often, the gleam of dentist's intervention would so stun the recipient that a reciprocal smile was always forthcoming. It worked this time.

'Hi I'm Catriona' I nodded and took her hand. 'Would you like a drink?'

'Bushmills, double.'

I ordered for the pair of us. A tenner lighter, my wallet flopped back sadly into its pocket, hoping that was all for today. We drank the whiskey and arranged to meet next morning at the quay. She owned a 14 ft Orkney longliner that she used to catch lobster and crab, making a small but significant living during the season. The boat was painted in saltire colours and named after her mother, Naomi Maxwell, who had funded it with a lottery grant when that ubiquitous game of chance had hit the Maxwell's to the tune of fifty thou. I didn't know all this then, just that this lovely girl was giving up a day to ferry me across the sea to Anthrax Island.

The pub did bed and breakfast, and I tumbled into the slightly pink nylon sheets on the single hard bed that had never seen a decent mattress, let alone a memory foam one.

Chapter Two

The Bushmills had anesthetised me, and I fell into an untroubled sleep. The last I should get for some time. But again I was blissfully unaware of this!

A hot Scottish summer morning greeted me. Not a cloud in the sky, not a breeze to ruffle the placid harbour waters of Laide. The village, hamlet more like, spread out along the main road and so missable that hardly a car stopped, as they all sped through with their touristic eyes fixed upon the granite peaks of An Teallach in the distance. A pity, for Laide is a pretty wee place.

After a full Scottish: black pudding, bacon, beans, sausage, two eggs, fried bread and enough cholesterol to set off the alarms in the heart unit in Ullapool Hospital, I staggered down to the quay. The Naomi Maxwell was tied up by the wharf, but of Catriona there was no sign. I hung about like a piece of wind-blown lint, until after a few minutes she came down the hill carrying a shopping bag. None of your plastic crap that takes a million years to decay, this one was of unbleached hessian with the logo of a well-known whole food shop in Glasgow emblazoned across the front, and the legend "walk soft upon the earth" written across it in indelible black ink. Fat chance of saving the planet that way, still every little helps.

'What's in the bag?'

'Just a bit of lunch. Cheese. Olives, bread, strong lager!'

I nodded thoughtfully. We pushed off from the quay and Catriona fired up the 15 h.p. Mercury that hung off the back of the longliner like a colostomy bag. With a roar the engine caught, and smooth as you like she swung us out to sea towards the island. Less than a mile off shore, it is a low-lying little bastard with a hill at the west end approx 500 feet high. Covered in bluebells in the spring and used as summer grazing, the island is so seldom visited that any wild life is tame as tame. Not that there's much; rabbits supposedly and a couple of sea eagles. But they weren't there today. It's only half a mile to the island so we decided to circle round and approach from the seaward side. No point in having the ladies of Laide watching us through binos. Behind the island, where the relentless Atlantic pounds the granite, the cliffs rise up about 500 ft or so. The bottom section is peppered with sea caves through which the roar and scent of the sea smashes its inexorable way, and has done for millennia. On this calm day we got close up, and a small pebble beach led us inward where we dropped anchor and waded ashore. Ahead a deep cleft in the granite led us on into a natural sea cave fashioned over aeons. Ahead, deep against the rear wall and above the high water line, a pile and plethora of metal litter, blue polypropylene rope and all the crap that gets washed up from the ocean. Quite a colourful extravaganza of litter: floats, fenders and bits of orange fishing net.

'Will you look here Davie?' She called me over, and squatting down in front of an ancient rusty five-gallon drum gave it a twist with her foot so I could read what was left of the stencilled writing on it: '1942. Ministry of War. DANGER. Chemical powder. Keep clear'. There were three drums like this. More worrying were the other ten or so fifty-gallon drums neatly stacked at the back of the cave, each with its lid firmly in place and each with the radioactive symbol heavily stencilled on the drum.

'Fucking Christ, Catriona, this looks like someone's stashing radioactive waste here on the island. Think about it. No one goes there. The locals bravado still stops them coming over to visit, only a few journos from London who have been charged £700 for the privilege of landing on the landward side of the place ever come here, and they don't know the difference between a seagull and a sea toilet.

She looked at me and nodded. Out o here and we left in a hurry.

Back in the boat we pushed out to deeper waters and continued our circumnavigation, finally beaching where everyone else did. A pleasant two-hour walk across the island led us to the high ground where the strong lager, and cheese and olives got eaten. I wandered away to have a pee, and just down out of sight of the top noticed some raw marks on the low-growing turf and heather mix that makes up the vegetation in these parts. Looking more closely it was obvious that someone had been digging the soil away in this place, and quite recently. Further down the slope another deeper scar was revealed as a fuller depth of topsoil had been discovered. I shouted back at Catriona.

'Some bastard's been digging the soil away here.' She came bounding down the hill and knelt to examine the holes.

'Aye you're right. They did say some Scottish terrorists had sold some soil to Al- Qaeda some time back, but most people just laughed at that. This looks more recent. This year I'd say.'

We gathered our things and walked back down to the boat discussing the likelihood of anthrax spores still living in the soil, and other such earth shattering ideas.

Back on the mainland and after an exchange of address, which showed me her mother lived just over the hill, and Catriona also had a Loch Lomond hideaway.

My Gorbals, cold-water flat raised an eyebrow.

'Didnae think any puir soul still lived in such squalor anymuir.'

'Wait till you see it girl, 'tis the Tardis personified,' I lied.

She waved me off on my beemer and blatting the engine like some boy racer, I burnt rubber and scattered gravel as I revved up to forty and away down the road Glasgow bound.

The A852 winds its way like a demented ribbon across the highland starkness and eventually joins the A87 at Nostie - a nasty wee roadhouse sort of a place where a burger and chips can be bought in an eighties style roadhouse, with a car park big enough to cater for every truck in the highlands. The pot-holed surface made of that famous Scottish road building material crushed dust, stretched out ahead like a grey undersheet on an unwashed bed. Empty, apart for a black windowed Range Rover, mud spattered and dully gleaming on its own in the huge lot. I drew up and took off my helmet. A slight cold drizzle swept across the car park as I walked up to the double teak doors that led into the well-lit vestibule. The teak-clad walls had several gold-embossed testimonials from the architects, builders, burger suppliers and other worthies who had managed to get round the planning restrictions for this development in the Highlands, and consequently had made a killing.

The main dining room was strangely deserted except for a table under the window where three men sat. These must be the Range Rover occupants, I thought. Nodding a greeting and getting nothing back but a blank stare I wandered over to the counter. A spotty-looking lassie, with her lank hair pulled back from her blank looking face, was idly wiping the counter.

'Mug of tea and a veggie burger and chips please,' my usual fast food order. Miss Congeniality behind the counter raised her eyebrows,

'Dinae have any burgers left.'

'Well what have you got?'

She pointed half-heartedly at a withered cheese sandwich curling itself up in humiliation in the chill cabinet.

'We got a deep fried mars bar.' Her eyes lit up at the though. 'You could have that with chips!'

'No thanks, just the tea please.'

I got a mug full of brown liquid and took it over to one of the thin formica tables surrounded by thin formica chairs and sat down. I looked across at the other occupants. What an unsavoury looking crew. Maybe my jaundiced eye and hungry belly was ordering my senses, but two of the three were heavily unshaved and decidedly Arab looking men; each with a gold earring and several gold teeth. They dressed in over-tight polyester suits with stripped shirts and thin ties. Their elaborately shod fee, in shiny black pointed-toe shoes, moving in time to the music from their iPods. The other man was a different thing all together: bulky and over six-foot with a belly swaying out over his waistband. His greasy grey hair swept back over a sweating lard-coloured face. His hairy hands like spiders lay poised on the table as if to pounce on anyone idle enough to come within their reach. I turned away.

'Hey Laddie,' he raised his eyebrows.

'What?' I asked.

'You've been on that Anthrax island. I seen you there.'

'Bollocks.'

'I'm warning you. Don't write or tell any one what you saw or where you've been. Or it'll be the worst for you. Capice?' He smiled. If a shark's smile can be called a smile. His filed teeth seemed to catch the light and shimmer like cut diamonds in the light of the dining room. Now normally when someone goes to the trouble of addressing a complete stranger, the niceties are usually involved. A bit of politeness and quiet interest in what the stranger might have to say, but not with this lot.

He summoned his bodyguard and they left. I sat thoughtfully drinking my brown liquid. No point in denying it I felt shaken. First, the discovery of the toxic waste then the removal of the top soil followed by this warning from Mr Unsavoury. What was I to make of all this? I put my helmet on and walked out into the car park. The Range Rover was gone. I'm blessed with a photographic memory and I could remember the numberplate of the vehicle; just to back up the memory though, I transferred it into my note book. Once I was back home I had every intention of finding out whose car that was. The drizzle had set in with a vengeance and so I set off into the teeth of it. Night was falling or a demi-dusk was swirling across the road. It was difficult to tell through the murk of the rain. I blatted down the road keeping below the legal limit for though there was no traffic the conditions were awful. I was riding along the shores of Loch Duich. To my left the hills rose high and steep, to my right the loch side fell away to nothing. I passed a forestry track. Suddenly, out of nowhere, twin headlights blinded me and the six-cylinder roar of a Range Rover engine screamed warning. The next thing I knew I was flying. The bike a-tumble behind me as I cartwheeled over and over down the rocky scree and into the cold waters of the loch. Helmet, snatched from my head. Warm liquid – must be blood coursing down my face and mouth. I fell into and out of consciousness. Above me on the road I could see the silhouette of the car that had hit me. Two of the occupants got out and came down the bank. They found me, and with a callous disregard for the niceties in life started in with the pointy-toed shoes kicking me into unconsciousness. I just heard a voice say in well-modulated Scottish tones, 'You're a wee toolie and your deed the next time I sees you!' A final kick to the head finished me off and I knew no more.

Not dead, but not far off. The cold loch water lapped against my chin and I was hard- put not to swallow it. Needn't have worried. Highland loch water, best in the world, full of minerals and bacteria strained through a sheep's lower intestine.

I came too in the curtain-shaded quiet of a hospital room. At least, that's what it seemed like. I couldn't move because my leg was in traction and my arm was half <u>cocked around a former</u> and heavily plastered. A drip bottle-fed me NHS nourishment and I was duly grateful. I groaned. It was supposed to be a bright and consequential question like; What happened? Where am I? But it came out like the last sigh of the last inhabitant on the face of the planet. It was enough. The door opened and two people came in. The man dressed in hospital whites with heavy round eye lenses peered at my stats, whilst the woman in a nurse's uniform bustled forward and checked my limbs.

'You're a lucky laddie. Another half hour and you would have floated off to Nivarna! Ha ha! Aye, twas just as well Jock and his mates were on an early fishing trip.'

I blinked. He continued. 'They saw your helmet floating in the shallows, then your bike lying on the shingle, then, lastly they found you. By Christ, you'd taken some punishment. What happened?'

I tried my best to give a factual account of my beating at the hands of those Arab goons, but the effort was too much and I slipped away into darkness again.

Some time later I surfaced, feeling better and able to croak. They gave me water and let my arm down from its restriction. This time there was a third man in the room. He wasn't such fun: Sergeant Mac Aleish from the Kyle of Lochalsh Constabulary. More used to dealing with salmon poachers and the occasional cannabis infringement amongst the disaffected youth of the highlands than full blown attempted murder. So my story left out the Arabs and the deliberate attempt to run me off the road. With hindsight I wished I'd come clean and left it all in the hands of the paper-work boys, but oh no, some dark and devious notion far back in what passed for my brain made me keep all this to myself.

My story revolved around not knowing the road, skidding on some gravel and running off the safe tarmac onto the very steep and rocky shore. My bike was total trash recovered to the local garage where in time my insurance company would inspect it and offer me a pitiful sum for the remains. I felt like weeping. Luckily, the paramedics who collected my body from the shore had the presence of mind to bring along my bike panniers, and amongst the sodden mass of dirty knickers and soiled tee-shirts my notebook remained intact and curiously dry.

After three days on my back and the bruises and cuts had started to heal, they let me get up to sit in the day room of The Kyle of Lochalsh Hospital, along with the chemo patients and the very obese gastric by-pass case who would insist on more food each time the trolley came round. It turned out that my leg was not broken. just badly sprained, and after an initial pain-filled half-hour when they removed the plaster and I'd finished swearing at the very pretty Fiona who had cut the plaster off, I started to make a good recovery. By the end of the week I was chafing at the bit. So I called Catriona.

'The number you called has not been recognised, please try again.' I tried again and again just to get the same reply. Then it dawned. She'd given me a wrong number in order to see off the useless freelance journo and leave the way clear for some hunk more suited to father her children. Then I had the brilliant idea of emailing her. Within minutes of sending a mail she had replied. 'So nice you bothered to get in touch, where are you.? More developments on your story.' I mailed her back with a résumé of what had passed since last we'd met. Her next message ordered me to get ready to leave: I was invited to convalesce at her home by Loch Lomand. Who could refuse - and within an hour I was waiting good as gold with my tongue hanging out, like that puppy I had been once before in the pub at Laide when first I cast eyes upon the heavenly Catriona.

Well the day passed, and no girl. But the enforced rest did strengthen me a bit and by the time they'd sent out for fish and chips and a huge plate of fresh-caught hake, and some well-cooked golden-wonder chips had made their way down into the ever open maw I call my belly, I was in a forgiving mood, and anyway, I then had a sleep. Restorative or what!

Chapter Three

S he never showed up until the next morning. Some of the gilt had worn off the gingerbread, but not much. As I ate my NHS porridge: a tiny bowl full of a smooth grey mixture that owed its origins more to wallpaper paste than the prince of grains, into the day room she came. Dressed in faded blue jeans and with her hair piled on her head, she looked beautiful. I told her so, she blushed I think, though she had a high colour.

'What took you so long?' asks I.

'Och, you know the wee boat doesna' go quicker than six knots.'

'Shit, Catriona, you haven't come all this way in the boat?'

'Well what else. I couldn't swim here.'

'Does that mean we're on our way south by sea?'

'Yes, we'll make a sailor of you yet!'

'But it must be hundreds of miles.'

'Aye a few hundred.' She grinned her wicked grin. 'We'll be able to get to know one another!'

I felt a bit sick. It's not that I mind the sea, in fact I quite like it, but I'm an air sign and air and water don't usually mix. I swallowed, and grinned a sickly grin up at her.

'So, my braw wee lad shall we go?'

15

Thanks to a pair of borrowed NHS <u>ali</u> crutches I was soon hopping down the path outside the hospital on my way to the quay where the Naomi Maxwell was tied up. We stopped to buy some provisions. Bread, cheese, peanut butter and more importantly a bottle of Bushmills. Then there she was, hove to against the wharf. Catriona had thoughtfully covered the fore deck with a tarp, which gave shelter from the storm and offered a useful space for terrified mariners to crawl into. We climbed aboard. In the makeshift accommodation, two sleeping bags were laid out on an air mattress and across the thwart in the fore peak, a double burner camping stove.

'Must get fuel,' she said and jumped back onto the quay. Taking the red petrol can in hand she was gone about ten minutes. Gave me just time to stash my saddlebags and start to get comfy. The day was calm, thank Christ. I didn't relish my first full day as a mariner on the likely weather one gets in the Highlands in summer.

We cast off. Catriona pressed the tit on the outboard and a satisfying deep bellow echoed up around he walls of the harbour.

'Plot a course for Mallaig, Davie,' she ordered. Complete confusion overcame me. Mallaig, Mallaig. It might as well have been Timbuctoo, except you can't get there by sea. Almost you can't get there by land!

'How ?' I screamed.

'Satnav of course. Put the name Mallaig into the machine and it comes up with a course. Follow that course and eventually you arrive.'

I shook my head in wonderment and did as she said. Quick as a flash the thing started bleeping and then spewing out some printed matter. I read it out to her.

'Due south. Twenty miles.'

She nodded contentedly. Even I felt the first stirrings of hope. Twenty miles, not far, shouldn't take long! The feelings of anxiety that were consecutively tightening and loosening my sphincter gave way to a feeling of calm enjoyment as we moved off down the Sound of Sleet. Other boats were on the water. Some special white plastic gin palaces crewed by expensive-looking men in blazers and deck shoes. An old carvel built cob with a very faded red sail, and a wild-haired hippy at the tiller raising his hand in greeting as we forged past. I started to feel like one of the fraternity of the sea, and grinned back at him. The weather was benign, a flat oily swell with no danger in it kept on coming under the hull of the boat. The sun blazed down. Catriona smiled out of her green eyes, I smiled back.

'Tell me, what of these Arabs that ran you off the road?'

'I wish I knew. I haven't had time to do any research on them yet. Anyway, my laptop got damaged in the accident and I need access to my pc at home.'

'I've got a laptop here, up in the cuddy. Here, take over the tiller and I'll look a few things up.'

She handed me the rudder, and swung past into the forecastle of the boat. After a wobbly blip whilst I fought with the direction of the boat, I got it under control obeying the principle that a little swing on the tiller produces a large swing on the sea.

'Keep the compass on south,' she called as she rummaged in a waterproofed locker under the thwarts, finally producing a laptop bag. She plugged into a p.v.cell that was fixed half way up the mast and after minutes she called back to me, 'What was that number plate again?'

My brain whirred and then, 'HTZ 789.'

She entered the number. 'University of Glasgow. Registered to the Dept of Arabic Research. In the name of the Director: Mohammed Al Arabi.

'Any address given?'

'No, but there is for the Department.' She read off an address that was right in the heart of the Uni. Campus.

'Now this is interesting. It says here that the bulk of the funding for this dept is given by the Peoples Republic of Libya.'

'Gaddafi,' I breathed.

'Yes, and there's a list of names and addresses of the researchers and graduates working in the Department. There's about a dozen of them, all Arabs, mostly all Libyans.'

'They can't all be Gaddafi loyalists.'

'No, but those clowns that gave me the boot certainly were.'

'Tell you what, though, barrels of toxic radioactive waste. Anthrax spores. It adds up to a dirty bomb! Didn't that maniac Gaddafi threaten to hurt the west? He's got long-range rockets capable of hitting Paris. What if he intended to launch a rocket attack on the West and the warheads contained a mix of radioactive waste and anthrax spores? He could kill millions!'

'Yeah, but it's only supposition. We need hard proof, and how are we going to get that?'

'Break into the research faculty and then into their computers. There must be some evidence there surely?'

'Well, I don't need to go to their offices to look at their computer.'

'Oh, why, can you hack their pc?'

'Of course. I didn't get a first in computer science for nothing you know.' She grinned her wicked grin again. 'What was the name of the top dog in that research unit?'

'Al Arabi. Mohammed al Arabi.'

'I'll see what comes up.' Her fingers flew over the keyboard. The laptop whirred.

'Interesting. He's been in the country three years. Mostly at the uni. But before that he worked at....' her voice trailed off. 'Oh shit! Before that he worked at Porton Down only as a porter for sure, but that gave him entry to some of the most sensitive chemical warfare secrets in the UK'

She looked over at me and screamed out. 'Hard aport, port your helm for Christ's sake or we're on the rocks!'

I have to say I'd been far away in a head trip and not paying attention to where we were going and the bows of the boat were within feet of some oily looking mollusc-encrusted rocks that had suddenly reared up out of the sea bed.

'Oh shit and bollocks!' cried I as I frantically swung the tiller left. Thank God the boat responded and just scraped the rock leaving a nasty gash along the wooden side.

Catriona glared at me.

'Will you be more careful with my boat. Pay attention when you're on the tiller will you!'

I nodded, admonished, and settled back to keeping a rigid southerly course by the compass. Catriona went back to the computer and no words passed between us for some time.

Our course took us past the wonderfully named Eigg, Muck and Rhum islands and down past Ardnamurchan point into the sound of Mull. A beautiful, some would say the most beautiful, part of the islands off the west coast. The three oddly named islands inhabited since time began and early man first gathered sea food along these shores; Eigg, Rhum and Muck had been privately-owned playgrounds for the rich and super rich. But times change, and some years back the inhabitants of these islands were able to throw off the shackles of ownership and buy the estates for the communal good. We were heading for Oban where I had agreed to stand her a dinner for having damaged the Naomi Maxwell. I felt contrite for sure and anyway I wanted off the briny and back on dry land as soon as poss. However, it was another four hours before we were safely berthed in the harbour at Oban. The Harbourmaster waived the mooring fees once he realised it was Catriona's boat tying up, and she had introduced him to me as Uncle Angus. So that was a perk. Every little helps in the constant battle to stay solvent. My reluctant wallet would hardly release its cash card, and with much moaning, I was able to extract £100 from the hole in the wall. We made our way to Mac Murdo's Fish bar and Restaurant where Catriona had a huge fresh sea bass and I went for some lovely Atlantic haddock, fresh caught that day and gently steamed in milk with fresh samphire. Now this was gourmet eating at its best and after a half hours' noshing we sat back replete, greasy chinned and grinning.

'By God, that was good,' I said feelingly. She just grinned the grin.

'Come on Davie my lad, back to the boat. We've got an early start in the morning; there's still a few miles to go.'

After a double Bushmills, we tumbled into our sleeping bags and within seconds I was deep in the arms of an uncaring morpheus, and Catriona was the same.

Chapter Four

Day two on the water looked to be a repeat of the one gone before: a high cirrus cloud base wisping across the blue of the firmament. Some time after dawn we cast off from Oban Jetty and with the rightful owner at the tiller, headed out for the Crinan Canal; another twenty or so miles due south. The day grew hotter and hotter still as the faint breeze was killed by the rising temperature. A pod of dolphins kept pace with us jumping high out of the placid swell as if playing some game. By midday we were both sweltering under some home-made hats Catriona had fashioned from handkerchiefs. Looking very like the John Cleese character, I sat and trailed my hand over the side. There was little difference in temperature between the water and blood heat.

'Throw a spinner line over, Davie; see if you can catch some mackerel for our tea!'

I rummaged around in the locker and found a reel wrapped around a thick piece of driftwood. At intervals along the line there were wicked looking hooks, each one with a neat piece of feather flying beside it. I undid the line and cast it into the sea. The boat's motion helped carry the line backward. Lying there, like the ancient Mariner, I felt the lure of the sea seep into my soul.

The line started to jerk and move of its own. I pulled it in, We must have passed through a shoal of mackerel, for before long there were ten beautiful fat green and grey specimens lying in the boat.

'Let the rest go Davie. You'll only be able to eat five, believe me.'

I unhooked the lucky survivors and slipped them back into the water to swim again. A quick lesson in gutting fish and I was as equipped as any Arbroath fishwife to take on a new career

'We'll cook these once we're through the Canal.' She cast a knowing eye up at the sun. 'Maybe three or four this afternoon!'

The Crinan Canal was built in the 19th century to enable a shortcut through to the booming city of Glasgow, used by the puffers and commercial vessels till the trade started to fall away and now utilised by holiday sailors and the occasional fisherman. It cuts a huge slice off the journey time and it's a beautiful way to go – especially if you've got a beautiful green-eyed companion by your side telling you the history of the place, and an anticipation of some freshly caught mackerel to come. We passed through Cairn Baan and down through Lochgilp Head before we tied up on the banks of the waterway. Catriona fired up the stove and I cooked the mackerel. A dab of butter, salt and pepper, and within minutes that smoky fishy smell that accompanies all fried fish frying, wafted over us. The fish was superb. Catriona was quite right, I could hardly eat five. But five I managed, and with my stomach distended sat back against the thwart and gazed out at the countryside.

'My God, I feel fatter than a fried fish fryer has any right to feel.'

'Well, you would eat five you greedy dog,' and she gave me a playful push. I pushed back. Push and shove and added laughter plus a bit of water throwing inevitably brought us into one another's arms, and it was with great dexterity that we started to kiss. Her mouth was tender and open and her tongue licked back and forth across mine. Our energy levels increased in proportion to our ardour until she said, 'Enough for now Davie, we don't want to use all this up so soon.' My head spun and my eyes glazed. A huge erection throbbed manfully down below but with some restraint I pulled myself together and back into the real world.

'OK, OK, enough for now!' I gave her the benefit of the Davie boyish grin that can, and has, charmed women before. 'So, how much further till we get to your home in the woods?' I knew she had a place deep in the wooded forest above Ardentinney: a small village that relied on tourism and agriculture. What I didn't know till later was that it was an Eco round house, built by herself from scavenged and found materials, without planning and only connected to any modern facilities by photo voltaic panels and a small wind generator. A compost toilet for waste removal and a half acre veg patch completed the ensemble. Sounded like total heaven to me, and the remembrance of her kisses filled me with a joy I had rarely known before. I was falling for this woman with a vengeance, and I didn't care, in fact I relished it.

'About another two hours on the water and then an hour by the bike into the woods. We'll be there by dark.'

'Bike, what bike? A pedal cycle?

'No you daft bugger, a Cossack outfit I keep for getting about to buy food and other bits and bobs.'

'Oh brilliant. I absolutely love those sidecar set ups. Has it got reverse?'

'Of course; that's the reason I got it in the first place.' She enthused. 'It's well built, like a tractor actually. And top speed's only fifty, fifty five, but after six knots in the boat. it's as fast as the Flying Scotsman!'

'So where do you stash the boat when it comes to it.'

'Och, the Laird lets me use a boat house he owns right by Loch Long. I keep the bike in there when I'm out in the boat and vice versa.'

'So what Laird's this who lets you use his boat house and turns a blind eye to your house in the woods?'

She looked a bit sheepish I have to say, and then it came out. 'My brother!'

'Your brother!

'Aye, my brother: the Rt. Honourable Sir Angus Strachen Bart. A beautiful bloke who owns half the land between Strone and Ardentinney.'

'How much would that be then?' My natural aversion to landowners seeping out of my mouth like an oily rag soaked in vitriol.

'Not sure, but round about sixty thousand acres!'

'What? Sixty thousand acres? By Christ Catriona I can hardly believe it. Have you anymore secrets to tell. A million in the bank? A luxury yacht in the Bahamas?' My voice had taken on the hectoring tone I found so intimidating when people had criticised me for the slightest thing. The hard jealousy and desire to destroy the enemy that the class struggle had engendered in me for many years surfacing before me like a rotten snake skin sloughed off to lie like poison between us.

She shrugged and I felt a cold wind come between us.

'Back in the boat, we've still a distance to go!'

I climbed aboard and silently now she gunned the outboard and set the little craft in the direction of Ardentinney.

I felt like a shit. What right had I to criticise this young woman, whom I had started to fall in love with. An accident of birth had thrown her into the aristocracy in the same way an accident of birth had thrown me up against the rat-infested walls of a cold-water flat in the Gorbals.

'Listen, Catriona, I'm sorry for what I said. There's no excuse for it and I apologise.' She looked up at me from her place by the tiller. I could see tears in her eyes.

'Yes, well, it's not my fault. He's not my true brother anyway. He's my mother's first husband's offspring. I'm as poor as the proverbial church mouse and everything I've got I've made myself or fought for myself. Anyway, I appreciate the apology and you're forgiven.'

The sun came out and, with her green eyes smiling, grinned again with that special warmth. I lent across the tiller and kissed her. She kissed me back, and I knew all was good in the world.

We talked about the Libyan situation and the general consensus seemed that we should visit the research facility at the University and see what we could glean from a personal visit. For sure, a personal look at their computers and a rummage through the paperwork wouldn't come amiss and might throw up some valuable facts we could rely on later.

'We need someone to keep an eye on Gruinard Island. They may try and remove the toxic waste.' I said.

'Oh that shouldn't be a problem. I'll call my Ma and get her to stake out the place. She only lives just over the hill. She is a wildlife illustrator and she's always out and about sketching. You can see the Island from her kitchen. She should be able to monitor any boat activity. Once we get home, I'll plug my mobile in and call her.'

We had entered a busy shipping lane as the Sound of Bute gave way to the Firth of Clyde. Boats of all sizes and classes appeared on the water. Huge bulk carriers three hundred yards long, covered like armoured lizards with containers from China and the Far East. Trawlers back from the Atlantic with cod and haddock aboard. Pleasure craft worth hundreds-of-thousands of pounds with their spinnakers up as they tacked and frolicked in the evening sun; their Helly Hanson-dressed deck hands with deck shoes costing more than Catriona's house, slapping down on the gleaming decks of the acres of whitened teak that made up only a partial cost of these millionaires' playthings. Not that I was jealous, far from it. My philosophy was, less things to own less worry to have, and that had stood me in good stead all my life. No house, no money in the bank, now no motorbike. But I did have the girl. I gazed fondly over at her. She stuck her tongue out in a friendly manner and concentrated on steering the small boat through the ever-thronging roads that led up to Glasgow. We threaded our way through the stream, Dunoon to Port, Grenock to Starboard and up into the quieter waters of the approach to Loch Long. To our left the heavily wooded slopes of Stonghullin Hill reached out its green tentacles to embrace and hold us. The village of Ardentinney hove into view. Catriona pulled on past it, until some mile or so further up the loch a wooden boathouse nestled in the shelter of a wooded creek. Swinging the tiller hard a port she brought our boat into shore and straight into the open mouth of the boathouse. In the dim gloaming I could see that it was a more substantial building than I had first imagined.

Although wooden-sided, the bottom courses were well-laid substantial stone and the berths were big enough for two boats the size of The Naomi Maxwell. Running round the berths were hard standing and at the top of the shed, well out of the way of any water, stood a three-years old Cossack sidecar outfit. It gleamed in its black and gold livery. The sidecar was on the correct side to make it legal on the roads and generally it looked in very good order. The sidecar was a substantial metal structure with an all weather tarp over it to keep out the rain. The huge spoked wheels on the sidecar lent it certain strength and fixed to the top of the sidecar was a spare wheel.

I could see a fifty-gallon tank of gasoline on a metal stand with a padlocked pump. Tools were neatly stacked against the wall over a metal workbench. All neat and tidy.

'My God, Catriona, this is good. You've everything you need to keep both boat and bike maintained.'

'Aye, I hope so. Give us a hand to tie the Naomi up, and then we're off to the House in the Woods. I jumped out onto the quay and caught up the painter. I Pulled the boat into the side and carefully secured her against the wharf through the metal ring that hung there. Catriona was doing the same thing at the stern and before long the longliner was going nowhere.

We transferred our belongings into the sidecar and I eased my six-foot two inches into the metal box. Bit of a squash, but manageable. Cossacks fire up on a kick-start and this one was a good 'un. A couple of preliminary petrol into carb thrusts and on the third poke she roared into life. Catriona had already opened the double doors at the top of the boathouse and we plunged out straight on to a hard stone-lined forestry track. Braking the bike, Catriona went back and locked the boathouse doors and then we were off. Feeling more than a little like Gromit sitting in the sidecar, I let the balmy, pine-scented air of the encroaching forest waft around me as Catriona gunned the engine of the Russian bike and we trundled away up into the wooded hills. We had gone about a mile when the tracks split. Taking a left hand she revved the motor to climb a fairly steep section of track. There ahead of us, in a clearing about an acre or so within a backdrop of old Caledonian forest pine trees and overlooking the placid waters of Loch Long below, stood The House in the Woods. Totally circular and one storey high, the dwelling blended into its surroundings. Two 15-inch diameter pine trunks set into the earth served as gateposts for the heavy oak front door that excluded entrance to the dwelling. A turf roof planted with native grasses local to the forest roofed the structure. Three p.v. cells set in the roof provided power for the 12-volt lighting system whilst a small, waterproofed shed beside the house held a bank of 12-volt batteries. Further along the lane a compost toilet downwind of the dwelling, and to complete the ensemble a shower room with solar panel heating. Higher up and on a prominence of the hillside stood a small boat wind generator.

'Welcome to The House in the Woods. Come in, take your shoes off and leave them in the porch.'

She unlocked the door. The key to which was stashed in a dead branch hollow in the nearest pine tree. We went in. It was still light enough to see the interior without the aid of artificial light, and I was blown away. One large circular room: about thirty feet in diameter. In the middle a Jotul wood-burning stove with a stainless chimney that rose up through the turf roof. The walls of the dwelling were made from thick willow strakes criss-crossed in the style of a yurt, and covered in oriental carpets and other exotic far-eastern materials. Either side of the entrance doorway two small glazed windows let in sufficient light to enable someone to prepare a meal at the heavy oak refectory table that stood near the wall. A stainless sink stood beside it with a waste pipe exiting the building through the wall. Opposite, against the wall, a double bed made from forest timber with a Cath Kidson design quilt and duvet thrown over it. Two stainless water jacks in the style of the travelling gypsies stood beside the sink. A pair of comfy old leather chairs in the club style completed the furniture. I looked down. The floor was of beaten earth, but so polished by the passage of many feet over the years that it was now as hard as concrete and as gleaming as copper. I suddenly realised why I had been told to take my shoes off. I gazed around this paradise with slack-jawed amazement.

'My God, Catriona, this is beautiful. You've done this by yourself?'

She nodded her head in a shy way.

'Thanks, I rather like it too. There's no planning on it mind, so if it gets sussed those bastard planners will most probably make me pull it down. It's been here five years and no one's said a thing. Plenty of folk know it's here, but they don't seem to mind. I got the idea from a friend in Pembrokeshire. She lives in a similar house at Brith de Mawr. Sadly she got caught by the authorities when her solar panels were caught on camera gleaming in the sunlight. Then it took her five years of bureaucratic shit and hassle before they gave her retrospective planning permission. Cost her £70 to build the house and £15000 to fight the planners. Luckily, there's a gang of low-impact livers all over the UK only too willing to put on gigs and raise money to help folk who run foul of the planners. This house was a bit more expensive than my friend's;

this one cost a hundred quid. Oh, that includes the wind genny. My friend's house became quite a cause célèbre when she got sussed: The School of Architects in New York wrote to Pembrokeshire County Council extolling the viruses of low-impact eco houses, and offered to dismantle it and ship it to the States as a prime example of the genre! Also St Fagan's, the museum in Cardiff, wanted it in their grounds for future posterity. I don't think either of them made a blind bit of difference to those wankers on the Council; "rules is rules you know". What hypocrite little shits: because they gave planning to a conservative millionaire M.P. to build an underground gin palace right on the cliff!' She laughed outright and I couldn't help but hug her and join in. What a woman: sailor, biker, home-builder, would her multi-faceted polymathism never cease!

'I'm going to phone my ma and organise her.' She plugged her mobile into a 12 volt lead and pressed keys. Within moments she was talking nineteen to the dozen, and in a few sentences had outlined all that had passed and what she wanted her mother to do. After a few pleasantries and a bit of lewd laughter she cut the connection.

'OK, she's going to look out for any boat activity round the island, no matter how big or small, and report back; phoning in here each day at 6 p.m. If we're not here and there's something to report she'll leave an answerphone message. Now, we need to plan our next moves.'

Chapter Five

I looked at her. Her intense green eyes gazed back at me. I needed some space to get to my flat and pick-up some things. Not least the huge and unwieldy Colt .45 that my father had bequeathed me from his time in the Western Desert in '42. Not that I'd ever fired it, and anyway; did I have ammo for it? Not sure. OK, it would be possible to acquire ammo. But it was the psychological comfort of a heavy weapon that was making me salivate. Also I needed my laptop and a change of clothing. Not to say all the paperwork to deal with the bike etc. etc.

I said, 'I need to go to Glasgow and visit my flat. I better go on my own. Need a few things. Change of clothes etc. Got to do some paperwork on the bike and pick-up a bit of cash. OK with you?'

'OK' she didn't seem phased. 'Tell you what, we'll meet up on the campus in two days' time in the student's uni. OK? And in between times I'll hack into their research data and see just what they're up to.'

'Can I take the bike?'

'No, it must stay here for us to use. I'll give you a lift to the ferry and you can get a bus, its only thirty miles.' I nodded again.

Dark had fallen, and she opened the front of the Jotul and lit the fire within. A warm fug filled the circular

31

room, and a light meal of cheese on toast with the ubiquitous Bushmills completed our evening. For the sake of propriety I shall gloss over the hours between supper and falling asleep in her arms, suffice it to say it was the most exciting thing that had ever happened to me. She seemed to enjoy it as well! We tumbled into her double bed and the Cath Kidson duvet had hardly been pulled over my shoulders than I was asleep.

Woke up with the sun streaming in like a hot mountain stream bathing me in its glorious warmth. The bed beside me was empty but still smelt of Catriona. Of the lovely girl there was no sign. Then from beyond the roundhouse in the direction of the shower room this melodious alto singing voice floated up. A pure on-key wonder: McCartney's Fool on the Hill, floating like a free spirit across the glen. I stretched in unabashed joy and swung my feet onto the beaten earth. She was just emerging from the shower with her long red hair loose down her back. She flung me a kiss and avoided my frowsty mouth. I darted into the shower and a blissful five minutes of solar-heated steam ran in rivulets upon my body. She's the only woman I know who'd willingly have Euthymol toothpaste in the place. Most 'ladies' have never heard of it. It's a man thing. But there on the shelf was the familiar green and white tube. Next to it an unopened toothbrush. I took full advantage. Back in the house, enticing breakfast smells were wafting about as I finished dressing, and there in front of me was a plate of fried eggs and tomatoes, a rack of toast and a large cup of Kenya peabury coffee. I ate substantially.

'I'll run you down to the Gareloch Head ferry. You can get a bus into town from there.'

'OK and I'll see you in the students' Uni in two days' time.'

'Yes, that should give me plenty time to check out these Libyans. My mobile number's here.' She read out her number, which I entered into my phone. That, in retrospect, was one of my better ideas.

Breakfast done, she fired up the Cossack and we sped down the track in the direction of the little ferry that crossed to Gareloch Head. It was only a chain drive flat-bottom boat too small for cars but perfect for foot passengers. I waved goodbye and watched her turn and disappear up the hill in the direction of the House in the Woods. My heart gave a little pang of regret. Why the hell did I want to go gallivanting off to Glasgow when I could rest in the arms of my beloved? Well I always was a stupid bastard!

The Ferry docked and I walked up the cobbled quay-side to the bus station. Buses left once an hour on the hour and I saw from my watch I had time enough for another cup of coffee. The waiting room in the bus station was the usual hell hole, with uncleared tables. Microwaved Cornish pasties guaranteed to give you heartburn, and an Arabic- looking man sitting behind dark glasses at one of the tables. His shiny patent leather winkle-picker shoes brought back the fear. But he had seen me. Straight away onto his mobile and after a quick call he legged it. I pretended I'd never seen him and ordered a brown liquid with a taste of curry about it. £2.50. The waitress offered a show of complete indifference when I quizzed her as to what poisonous variety of drink was this. Hardly able to finish it, I was just in time to board the bus into town.

An hour-and-a-half later the bus dropped me at the bus station near Sauchiehall Street and I got a local single decker to the Gorbals. My flat was on the third floor of a renovated tenement block on Norfolk Street; in typical Glasgow style, with three storeys and oriel windows, a bold chimney and a saucer dome. These had been refurbished in the great clean-out of the 80's, and very comfortable they were. Mine was owned and managed by the Council. A subsidised rent kept the other occupants sweet as they went about their drug-induced daily lives. Not their fault. Far from it, but severe deprivation and lack of opportunity had blighted a whole generation. Jockie, a Ralph C. Nesbitt look-alike down to the string vest and the can of strong larger, and this was early in the morning mind, shouted out a greeting.

'Hey ho Davie, lend us a fiver.' I shook my head and grinned at him.

'No way Jockie, you've got more money off the benefits than I'll see in a long time.' His drunk features laughed up at me and from his pocket he withdrew a wedge of money. Maybe £200 or so. Money he'd use between now and next benefit day to stay intoxicated and do a few deals on the street.

'I got a nice bit o smack here if you'd like it.'

I looked affronted. 'You know I don't do that.'

'Aye, more fool you,' and he cackled off into the basement area where he slumped against the wall to drink his lager.

I climbed the stairs. Needless to say, the lifts had stopped operating within a month of the refurb, and after having fixed them three times the lift company just kept putting an invoice into the Council every month for repairs that never got done. Just how folks made a living round here! When night fell in these parts, the good citizens retired to their flickering screens and the re-runs of Taggart. Whilst the real drugged-up living zombies of the streets took to their natural habitat and their natural drug dealing and twocking. More cars got burnt out here on the green sward of the Gorbals Green than ever did in Beirut on a Saturday night. The Police, hard put to earn a decent wage, were as corrupt as any police force anywhere, and a blind eye was turned to most of the Jocks and Moiras, some as young as eleven, who nightly rampaged through the mean streets.

Two stories more and my front door hove into view. It was open. I approached warily and pushed. The heavy frame swung in the air. Someone had forced an entry. Most probably with one of those police rammers used so ubiquitously on the telly. I stepped through the door into a vision of utter destruction. My home, such as it was, had been totally trashed. Every item of furniture had been slashed with a Stanley knife: all my collection of deco ceramics gathered over years at local car boots' lying smashed in pieces. Of my laptop and telly no sign. In the kitchen, even worse. Tins and jars had been emptied in a malicious melange of stickiness and poured indiscriminately over the tables and chairs and equipment. The toaster had then been turned on high until it blew a fuse. The bedroom had suffered a similar fate. My clothes ripped and torn lay scattered over the slashed duvet. They'd even gone to the trouble to up end the mattress and slash it apart and then break the slats on the bed. All I wanted to do was weep. Instead I got out my mobile and tried calling Catriona. No reply. So I sent a text instead. 'Home early, my flat trashed. Pick me up at ferry about six. Love Davie.'

I'd just finished sending that and was sitting with my head in my hands when I felt a very cold and very metallic gun barrel insert itself just under my ear.

'So you little shit you've come home early have you?' I screwed round to confront one of the Arab goons who had given me a good kicking the other day on the banks of the loch.

'Get up and no funny business. We're going somewhere you're not gonna like.'

He gave a cackle of maniac laughter and forced the gun barrel into my ribs. I staggered up and he frogmarched me out of the flat. Down the stairs and into the same black Range Rover. Déjà vu flashed before my eyes. The driver, the other goon, grinned nastily at me.

'Hi there Davie, nice to see you again. Mr Al Arabi wants a few words.'

He started the engine and we drove through the streets of Glasgow and into the butcher's district. This was an area waiting to be developed into bijou little apartments for Guardian-reading, middle-class Scots who were teachers or accountants or lower-echelon bankers. But at this time was still full of empty meat warehouses. These would have passed muster in a Sly Stallone film as a dead ringer for downtown Philadelphia. In fact a new movie was being made using just these very buildings. Martin Scorsese, I thought, a man who worshipped detail to such an extent that when he cast extras in one of his movies recently he made them wear period underwear and period shoes for many hours at a time. Bunion factor ten, as my female friends would have it. These thoughts flashed through my mind. I hoped I was in a movie, or at least in a nightmare. They pulled up outside a red brick building and hustled me inside. Through a huge double door and into a cavernous cold room with condensation dripping from the ceiling and a series of meat hooks operated by chain pulleys. They stripped my clothes off and shackled me to one of the meat hooks. With a leer my captor started to winch me upwards until I was dangling just off the floor with my arms stretched out above my head. A feeling of utter terror and loneliness descended on me. This is it, tortured to death by Arabs. My sphincter muscles gave way and I felt a trickle of warm urine flow over my legs. The Arab laughed.

'Now you tell what you know.'

'Nothing, you bastard.'

'Oh, but you do,' another more modulated voice joined in. The meat hook swung round to reveal Al Arabi holding a jockey whip. Suddenly he struck out and whipped the crop across my buttocks. The pain seared through me. Then again and again until I sobbed brokenly with the pain.

'No, no stop I'll tell you anything'.

He smiled. His diamond teeth glinting in the light of the unshaded light bulb.

'So what do you know of anthrax spores and the island?'

Chapter Six

Itold him everything I knew. I'd do anything to stop the pain. He struck out again. I writhed in agony. The shackle spun with my weight on it and by this time the torture had become more of a punishment, and a pleasure to Al Arabi and less than a means to extract information. Eventually I lapsed into unconsciousness and for a blissful time the pain eased. My mind was a whirl of conflicting emotions as I slipped in and out of consciousness. I seem to recall voices from a long way off shouting, and then whispering, and then nothing.

I came to – who knows how long I had been unconscious. Instantly the pain started as my buttocks and testicles flared with the agony of the beating. I screamed and I screamed. There was no response. The warehouse was empty, no sign of Al Arabi and his mates. I was still shackled, but by now my weight had dragged me down towards the floor and my body was suspended on the cold concrete. I tried to stand but my feet buckled under me. I could feel blood dripping from my nether regions and the pain flared uncontrolled and almost tipped me back into oblivion.

I managed to stand upright and take the weight off my arms. The shackles fell loose around the meat hook and by a supreme effort I was able to pull my chained wrists over the hook. It was only a moment of sweating terror to slacken the chain and remove it from my hands. My clothes lay in a heap on the sodden floor. Hastily I dressed. Still no sight or sound of my torturers. It was as if they'd never existed. I hobbled over to the heavy doors and pulled one open. A stream of light came bursting in. No-one in sight. The empty road outside stretched towards the bustle of the city. Like a wounded hermit crab, I scuttled sideways towards the light, and welcome society of warm human beings. At the end of the road a bus stopped and I got on. It took me back to Sauchiehall Street and civilisation. By the time I was back on the ferry, my shock and horror at my treatment had given way to a cold anger.

Waiting at the ferry stop was a sight that lifted me beyond the normal into the superlative land of the loved and loving: Catriona with a look of concern on her face and the wonderful Cossack outfit.

'What the Christ happened to you?' she gasped as she took in my sodden clothes and bruised body. I told her all. She acted all sympathetic and hustled me back to the sanctuary of the House in The Woods where a hot shower and plenty of calendula ointment lovingly applied to the burning fiery parts of me had me almost believing not much had happened. Until I tried moving. Whereupon the pain struck like red–hot needles.

'You'll need time to recover from this. Sit here and let me tell you what I've found out.'

I nodded thankfully and sank into one of the old leather club chairs.

'OK Davie my love.' This being the first time she had addressed me as such, brought a warm glow to my heart and went a long way to start the healing.

'This is what I've got. I hacked into their research computer, and needless to say its all innocence and light and gives nothing away, but their personal and private PCs are another thing altogether. Al Arabi is a top Libyan nuclear scientist with a connection to the Lockerbie bomber. The bloke they released last year from prison here in Scotland is his first cousin. He has been high up in the Libyan regime almost since day one, and he has the ear of Gaddafi himself. The other two are just goons. One is a Lieutenant Colonel in the hated Shalamis battalion and the other is his cousin. But get this. There is a paper in the file that lays out very neatly the whole of the plot they're involved in. Firstly, they were ordered to obtain anthrax spores from the island. Ship them to Libya where Al Arabi is going to supervise the manufacture of a dirty bomb, using them and that toxic radioactive waste they've got stored on the island. The plan is to use it in warheads in some of their long-range rockets. You know they're capable of reaching parts of Europe no trouble. We've still got some time. They're not due to move the yellow waste until the end of the month. Their facility in the desert is under attack from NATO warplanes and they're worried they'll have to move it all further inland to a site where they can complete the task without interruption.'

'How do they intend shipping the stuff from the island?'

'They've chartered a deep-sea trawler, The Rose of Trale, which is due off Gruinard on the 30th.'

'Are they up to a sea voyage like this; it's a long way to Libya from Scotland?'

'Oh yes, they've got the Captain of The Rose in their pockets. He used to be IRA, and received weapons from them in the 80's, now they're calling in the favours.'

'We need to be on that boat, or at least shadowing it. There has to be a way we can sabotage them.'

She shook her head. 'Tall order Davie, but there is one other thing we can try. We can hire a boat ourselves and shadow them down to the Med.'

'Whoa, that's a hell of a way. I know you're a sailor, but I'm not, and I can see dangers here that you might not.'

'Well, what are we going to do otherwise: report all this to the authorities? Who, MI6?'

'Yes, for want of a better.'

'Who do you know in MI6?'

'Well strangely enough….. The Laird.'

'The laird!' I almost jumped back in alarm. Here she was telling me that her step-brother was part of the secret establishment. Well what the hell. The game had moved on from a simple journalistic story to a major national crisis and time was up for shilly-shallying around.

'Christ Catriona, you kept that pretty secret. Yes, good thinking. We'll get him involved and then we can step back and lay our responsibilities at the government's door.'

'OK I'll call him. She plugged her mobile in to the p.v. panel and hit in a few numbers.

'Angus?'

'Catriona. Any chance I can come up to the Big House, I've got something important to talk to you about and a friend I want you to meet?'

'OK dear, see you in half an hour. Bye.' She put the phone down.

She gathered up all the paperwork we had acquired so far, and stuffing it into a brief case we climbed aboard the Cossack and set off northerly through the woods. After running through the old Caledonian forest, with ancient

Scots pines and Douglas spruce overhanging the road and past small lochans, we eventually came round a sweeping bend in the track to see ahead a 16th century Scottish castle, with round corner towers framing a three-storey middle section whitewashed,with a sweeping gravel drive leading up to the imposing double doors. There were quite a few of these clan laird houses in the Highlands; this was a particularly pretty one. The turrets caught the morning sun and the tiny, well-laid slates gleamed as if they'd just been cleaned.

'Camgorhan House,' said Catriona. 'Built in 1540 by The Lord of The Isles. Came in to Angus's family about 1603 as a gambling debt and been nestling there ever since.'

Jealousy sparked up in me again. I sniffed, 'Very nice, I'm sure!'

'Come on Davie, give us a break. We've got better things to do than fight a class war, Don't you think?'

She was right. The safety of Europe hung in the balance here, and I was pettily allowing my baser instincts free reign. She swung the combo to a stop on the gravel front and we climbed out. A scruffy looking hippie bloke about forty, forty-five with silver hair long and tied back in a ponytail, with an equally long and scruffy beard, came out of the house.

'Cat!' he cried, and flung his arms about her. Jealousy flared again. She pulled away and grinning said,

'Angus, this is Davie my particular friend. Davie this is Angus, Laird of all you survey.'

Angus! The object of my scorn! The man I had assumed would be dressed in tweeds with a couple of Labrador dogs at heel, turned out to be your 60's throwback dope-smoking, never washing, earring pierced, old hippie. I

stepped forward and shook his hand. 'Nice to meet you.'
The cliché tumbled out.

'And you, mate. Come in the schloss and have a
drink.'

We went into the baronial hall. About sixty feet long
with a hammer beam ceiling and highly polished slate
flags on the floor. A huge, open, light marble fireplace at
one end in which burnt a massive log fire; did nothing
to warm the place but looked great. The walls were
hung with trophies of the hunt: huge stags' heads and the
occasional otter or two. There were crossed claymores
and the accoutrements that go along with Scottish castles:
immensely long pikes of the weapon variety, and in a glass
case an immensely long pike of the fish variety with the
legend, 'Caught by Angus Strachen, aged 11 on Doon
Loch, May 2nd 1970. Weight 64 lbs'.

'Nice fish,' I said.

'Aye, 'twas a bit of a struggle to land it. It weighed as
much as me.' He laughed.

'Cat, you said you had something to talk about?'
She passed him over the briefcase and he pulled out the
contents.

'Neil!' he called, and a traditionally-dressed butler
appeared as if from nowhere. 'Three Bushmills, if you
please. Ice and water.'

'Aye Sir.' Neil backed away and was back in moments
with a silver tray upon which the whiskey stood. He
placed it on the table and discretely withdrew. It was early
for me to start on the hard liquor, but if the others were,
why should I deny myself? I took a slurp from the lovely
amber-coloured liquid.

Angus looked at us. 'Yes, we know most of this.
We've been monitoring this bunch of sharks for some

time. Didn't know they were moving so soon to get back to Libya with the spores though.'

'Can you help?'

'Well, unofficially, yes, but the government must not be seen to be involved with anything to do against Libya at the moment. It was hard enough getting a UN resolution for a no-fly zone. Any involvement on top and the Russians and Chinese call foul and the shit hits the fan; and who knows? Give me a mo. I'll make a call or two.' He left the room. Within ten minutes he was back.

'Are you prepared to sign the Official Secrets Act?'

I looked dubious. Was this the slippery slope down which my principles of fair play and no rendition were about to slide?

Catriona said, 'Well, I will if it means stopping these bastards. You should have seen what they did to poor old Davie.' She shot a sympathetic glance my way. The memory of it tipped me pretty quickly in the right direction.

'Aye, I'll sign.'

'OK Repeat after me with your right hand on this bible.' He spouted some words about the sovereign right of the UK to come after us and cut our bollocks off if we divulged anything we heard or saw from then on anywhere in the world appertaining to this story. We also signed a paper, which looked like our death warrant, which Angus scooped up and locked into a neat little domed casket.

'OK Catriona and Davie, you're now bona fide members of MI6. Non-attributable. If you get in trouble, we deny you. However, we'll fund a boat for you to shadow these Arabs to the Med., and some weapons and a bit of instruction in their use. But that's as far as we go.

Any involvement by us is strictly off the cards. Do you understand?'

We both nodded. It seemed so easy: one minute untrammelled citizens of the United Kingdom to come and go without let or hinderance; the next undercover and non- attributable spooks, skulking round the most dangerous bit of business to come anyone's way in a long time. I foolishly asked if we'd get paid! The Laird gave a hollow laugh. Not in money terms it seemed, though the gratitude of the country would be forthcoming if all went right. But we'd be forgotten if things went wrong.

International events were moving on apace with the Libyan rebels embarking on the end-game against Gaddafi and moving their pick-up trucks and anti-aircraft weapons into the capital. We decided that Al Arabi would most likely bring his planning forward, and determined to hire our boat and wait off the island of Gruinard to see what developed. Consequently we chartered a deepsea fishing boat from Clyde Marine, kitted out with the luxury of individual cabins and all necessary equipment to track the Arabs. The skipper that came with the deal was a tall competent looking Scotsman, with curly black hair and a thick beard, who went under the unlikely name of Cosmo Duke. He had years of deep-water experience, and a trip down to Libya was nothing to him. Later, a squat, over-muscled army sergeant and two squaddies came on board. Carrying a long wooden crate, they dropped it on the deck and proceeded to give Catriona and I a tutorial in the use of the weapons within.

AK 47s three, Walther PPKs three. A small crate of hand grenades, and enough ammo to start World War Three.

As we motored out of the Clyde on our way north we were instructed in the best use of the weapons. Sergeant

Nicholson took a hand grenade and explained that it had a five-second delay fuse on it so that once the trigger was released you had five seconds to throw it before it exploded .

'Course you can leave it late and use it like an airburst, but I don't recommend that. Not at this stage. Just pull the pin and throw the fucking thing'.

We nodded wisely.

'AK47, beautiful weapon, first developed by the Russians just after World War Two. Now the weapon of choice across the world by insurgents and armies for its ease of use, robustness and fire power. Takes this cartridge; comes in a magazine that clips here,' he showed us 'And you're ready to kill.' He pulled the trigger and a shocking noise erupted from the barrel. A herring gull was shredded in a bloody squarking mess as the two second burst sprayed wide over the quiet seaway.

'Bloody fucking Christ,' I swore in horror, as the fearsome weapon did its worst.

Nicholson picked up one of. the hand guns.

'Walther PPK.weapon of choice of James Bond and other unlikely heros. The gun Hitler used to top himself in the bunker. Easily conccaled, with a ten-round magazine. This is a little killer. Want a go?'

He held the gun out to me. Gingerly I hefted it in my fist. It weighed about a pound- and-a-half and as I got used to the sheer incongruity of a gun in my hand, a feeling of empowerment and strength started to wash over me. I pulled the trigger. Nothing. Tried again. Nothing.

Nicholson laughed. 'Safety off, dickhead,' and he flicked the safety catch. I squeezed the trigger. The little gun bucked in my hand and a flat crack echoed over the placid water. I flicked it on to semi automatic and touched the trigger. A sound like calico tearing farted out of the barrel, and stopped.

Nicholson said, 'There's only ten rounds in the mag, so I'd use it on single shot if I was you. Better use of ammo.'

I passed the gun over to Catriona who was much more competent with it, mastering the single shot and auto-fire as if she'd always had one of these stashed about her person. It turned out anyway that she was the small arms champion shot for the Highlands for the last two years, so had no need of training whatsoever. I hung my head in shame at my lack of macho achievement. Cosmo Duke, the skipper, showed as much skill as Catriona and before we had passed out of sight of the Clyde we all felt ready to take on anything the Libyans might throw at us! Famous last words. But we didn't know that then.

Chapter Seven

Our boat, The Mary Swift, was a converted Hull trawler, 75 ft long with a central wheelhouse and, thankfully, two small lifeboats slung on davits either side of the fish deck. She was owned by the Oceanic Research Group, and had been fitted out in some style a few years previous, to accommodate ocean scientists on their expeditions. Below she had a largish state room and three cabins. A galley capable of feeding the crew, who usually numbered four, but this time thanks to the paranoia of the British Government were restricted to Cosmo Duke, Catriona and myself. Her uprated 1000 horsepower diesel engine was capable of propelling her through the water in excess of 15 knots. Some sort of Q boat, I thought, as I investigated the galley. My anxiety had been overcome by my hunger, and as no one else seemed the least bit like making any grub, I felt it was down to me, or starvation. The larder was well-furnished with the basics, and before long I had rustled up some pizza dough with the quick-rise dried yeast I found in a drawer beside the sink. Onions and garlic sizzling in the pan, tomatoes from a tin and a liberal spreading of grated cheese; herbs and spices and a few black olives completed the pizza. Straight into the oven and half an hour later we sat at the table stuffing the delicious fare into our mouths.

I've never been so overwhelmed with praise as I was that evening, for it turned out that everyone was starving and I was the only forward thinker amongst them. Pig greed, on my part, really. Cosmo had to eat his slice up in the wheelhouse for although there was an autopilot on the boat, we were negotiating some dangerous reefs and shallow waters as we motored up the Sound of Jura.

Catriona called her mum and the conversation on microphone was most revealing.

'Hi Mum, any joy with boats around Gruinard?'

'Yes, Dear. A trawler appeared in these waters the day before yesterday; The Rose of Tralee she's called, and moved into position in the lee of the island. I went up the coast with my friend Rory in his boat and had a look at what they're doing.'

'You be careful Mum, no heroics. You understand.'

'Oh shush, it's the most excitement we've had round here since Mrs McDougal lost her false teeth,' Catriona's mum cackled with laughter.

'Anyway, we were able to see that they had loaded some yellow kegs onto a rib and were transferring them by winch into the hold of the boat. Once they'd finished, and I counted ten barrels, they up anchored and set off in a westerly direction.'

'No one saw you?'

'No, I'm pretty certain they didn't. Rory's boat has a low profile and it was quite misty.'

'So how long since they left?'

'Yesterday, about teatime.'

Catriona cut the connection and we sat and pondered this information.

'They've got 24 hours on us, but that may be to the good. Let's look at a chart, we may be able to intercept them further out to sea if we steam due west.'

Cosmo interrupted us. 'Hang on a moment, we must get rid of Sergeant Nicholson and his sidekicks. I'm sure they don't want a trip down to the Med.'

The soldiers looked a bit sheepish. 'I don't mind,' said one.

'No mate, it's back to Catterick Barracks for us, as soon as you can drop us on dry land.'

By now we were running through the Sound of Laing: a narrow waterway that separated the islands of Luing from Scarba and Lunga. About two miles wide, this channel was subjected to fast rips that shot through it each day as the tide came in and out. However it was only ten to twelve miles up the coast until Oban hove into sight, and we were able to dock and drop off the soldiers.

I took the opportunity to stock up on some Bushmills and other essential supplies and within a couple of hours the Mary Swift was on course southwest, past the island of Mull and out into the deep swells of the North Atlantic.

So far the weather had favoured us with a balmy Scottish summer haze across he heather-strewn hill of the islands and promontories we passed. But now suddenly from the west a dark, almost black, aspect to the horizon showed itself, and before long a spitting cold rain was beating on the glass of the wheelhouse window.

'Filthy weather forecast,' said Cosmo. 'Deep low, moving in from the west. Gale force winds. Seven on the Beaufort scale and heavy rain with sleet!'

'Shit,' I said and shuddered.

'Never fear Davie; these boats are built to take any weather. It might get a bit uncomfortable, but we won't sink. I hope.'

It was the last two words that worried the hell out of me; but there was nothing to be done but grit ones' teeth and go with the flow. I sought out Catriona and we settled in a corner of the state room. I flicked on the telly to get the latest news from Libya. The rebel advance was still progressing, although all the news was, where Gadaffi was, and would he pull some horror stroke with chemical weapons in a last-ditch attempt to beat back the rebels? I knew the chemical weapons bit was steaming south into the Med with a fanatical loyalist at the helm, and the terror of that potential outweighed anything I could see on the T.V. news.

The weather started to worsen, but the Mary Swift was built for sterner stuff than this day could throw at it, and although we were crossing directly into the face of the spume-filled combers, the hull rolled over them with a disdainful shake of its tail.

Cosmo called down from the wheelhouse on the intercom.

'I've got a boat ahead on radar. Could be The Rose. She's about five miles off and making a westerly run into the Atlantic. Shall we see if we can eyeball her?'

We climbed the companionway ladder and squeezed into the fug of the wheelhouse. Cosmo stood like a great black bear, his hands grasping the teak and brass wheel as the Mary Swift shouldered her way through the growing mountainous seas. On the radar screen a green blip moved slowly westward. Outside, through the monotonous back and forth of the windscreen wiper, nothing could be seen except the green and grey view of the sea. The waves each topped now with a startlingly white spray of foam, broke in a never-ending pattern. Streamers of spume blew back across the wave- tops as the Mary Swift plunged down into each trough and laboriously climbed again, only to plunge again as the grey combers filled our world with their natural majesty.

Suddenly, ahead, about a mile or more, I caught a flash of colour on the grey sea. A boat, not dissimilar from our own, but making much heavier weather of it. I could see that each time this vessel came to the top of a wave it almost broached-to as its stern was pushed inexorably down into the next trough.

Cosmo shook his head. 'Not enough power in the engine; must have a mechanical failure. If the weather worsens they might founder.'He pulled the short wave radio mike from its place on the bulkhead, and flicking the switch called into it.

'Ahoy, boat ahead. Do you require any assistance?' No answer came back. He tried again. Still silence.Once more he called into the radio. All of a sudden across the sea a flickering pattern of light flared from the stern of the boat ahead. The wheelhouse glass on the Mary Swift shattered as high velocity rounds came screaming in. Cosmo gave a coughing grunt and fell back against the chart table. The Mary Swift, deprived of a hand on the wheel, spun into the teeth of the gale and started to wallow into a trough. The cold wind and sheeting rain filled the wheelhouse.

'We're under fire!' I screamed. It was all I could think of.

Catriona grabbed the wheel and brought us back on course. Ahead the other boat vanished into a bank of mist.

'Look to Cosmo!' shouted Catriona. I pulled his body away from the chart table and tried to lay him on the floor. He was a big lad, and although he was still alive, several bullets had entered his body. He groaned and a trickle of blood oozed from his mouth. I examined him carefully, giving it the benefit of my St John's first-aid-course knowledge. He was wounded in three places. The worst being a deep purple wound just south of his spleen which dribbled blood. I tried to staunch the flow with a bandage from the first-aid box. The other bullets were embedded in his arm and shoulder and he was groaning with the pain. Meanwhile the shattered windows of the wheelhouse were letting in the worst of the weather.

Catriona said, 'We've got to get these windows fixed or we'll freeze to death.'

I volunteered to look for something to stop them up, however temporarily. In the hold I found a sheet of marine ply and a jigsaw. It was the work of moments to fashion a temporary structure that fitted into place across the shattered remains of the wheelhouse window. It cut out the light, but also the wind and the rain. The radar screen had been hit by the bullets and was useless. Luckily nothing else seemed to have been affected by the bullets. Catriona put the boat onto autopilot and we manhandled Cosmo down into his cabin.

'I don't like the look of that stomach wound,' I said sotto voce to her.

'Nothing we can do. We'll just have to see how things develop. Let's keep an eye on him and see how he is in the morning. Give him a shot of morphine for the pain. If he's no better, we'll have to make landfall and get him to a doctor.'

'Maybe we should do that now. He's got three bullets in him, and the longer it's left the worst it'll become.'

'You're right. No delay on this, we have to get him to a doctor.'

We ran back up to the wheelhouse and Catriona deactivated the autopilot and spun the boat back onto a reciprocal course. The weather was moderating slightly as we came down the Sound of Mull and berthed at Salen. Our google input had told us there was a cottage hospital there, and I had called ahead to warn them that a wounded patient would be coming to them for attention. Sure enough, as we touched land an ambulance with two paramedics was opening its doors and Cosmo was carried off and up to the hospital. We followed later. An efficient sister informed us that Cosmo was in the operating theatre, but that the state of his health was unknown.

A very pretty doctor in a white coat with the ubiquitous stethoscope approached us along the corridor. Having established our bona fides she told us that Cosmo was out of danger, though on a drip in intensive care and likely to remain there for the next few days. She sternly asked how it was he had been hit by three high velocity bullets. Such ordinance was not known to be that common in the Highlands and Islands. We both shrugged and acted innocent. She gave us an old-fashioned Scottish school-marm's look, and after telling us that Cosmo would be laid up for at least a fortnight marched off down the hall on her way to administer to the needy. The NHS is as efficient in Scotland as anywhere else, but if there's one thing they don't like it's mystery.

Chapter Eight

We looked at one another. 'We'll have to go on our own 'said Catriona.

I looked dubious. 'Do you think you could skipper us all that way?'

'Oh aye, it would only be a week at sea anyway. Good chance to teach you some sailoring!' she laughed. 'We need to get the window repaired and a new radar fitted and I don't want those bastards getting too ahead of us. Let's get off to the harbour and get busy!'

Down by the slipway where the Mary Swift was tied up were a series of net stores and other cavernous rooms built into the harbour walls, some of these had been converted into marine businesses. One with a bright painted blue and white signboard caught our eye. Jock Fisher. Marine repairs. Then in smaller letters beside this, "all types of boat repair undertaken". I opened the door. A weather-beaten man in his middle age, wearing a padded check shirt and blue jeans, sat at a computer in the office.

'Would you be Jock Fisher?'

He nodded. I explained our problems and he listened.

'OK, the window glass I can do straight away, the radar is a bit more difficult. I'd have to send to Oban for that and it'll take a day!'

We agreed a price, and within half an hour his pick-up truck duly loaded with the shatterproof-glass wheelhouse windows had pulled up beside the Mary Swift. He and his oppo were busy removing the old and fixing the new. There was a lot of muttering about blood and damage to the wheelhouse interior, but as both Catriona and I were disinclined to talk about it the muttering ceased, and then the only noise was that of the electric screwdrivers and saws. Jock had previously called a supplier in Oban and ordered a new radar. Luckily they were due on Mull that afternoon so we expected delivery. As good as their word a truck pulled into the quay area and a brand new Arpa Radar Pilot 1100 with lcd screen was off-loaded and installed in the wheelhouse of the Mary Swift, all within a couple of hours. We paid for it and Jock's repairs with Catriona's brother's credit card details, which seemed to be acceptable to the hard-nosed Scots who ran these small businesses; and as the sun started its inevitable descent towards the rim of the world we were chugging out along the Sound of Mull in a westerly direction. The weather had swung back to the placid, high summer midge-infested Scottish sweet-smelling-heather loveliness that made the country one of the best places in the world to live. I stared out of the new glass in the wheelhouse and wondered just what the next week or so might have in store for us!

Catriona was playing with the new radar set up, and every so often she gave a little cry of delight as some hitherto unknown feature of the thing manifested itself.

'Hey, this is good: it's got a fifty mile over-the-horizon view. I can't see those Arab bastards however; they must have made good time to be away off the radar.'

I was conning the boat after some instruction, and it was as easy as her little longliner when it came down to it. I felt like Captain Birdseye. The waymark navigation system gave a small bleep as if to reassure us that we were on the right course and we ploughed out into the deep Atlantic swell. We passed Malin Head and out into the vastness of the watery deep. Hundreds of fathoms of grey-green water under our hull, but it seemed we were as safe as houses. It felt like it. The incident with the shooting of Cosmo had shaken us, but MI6 operatives like us weren't phased by a little bit of gun fire!

Catriona was making a few calculations on her laptop and came up with the idea that if the opposition had got a twelve to twenty-four hour distance advantage over us and they'd been travelling at about ten knots they could be anywhere between 120 and 240 nautical miles ahead of us. No wonder we couldn't find them on radar! She then had the stunning idea of enlisting the Laird into the search, and within minutes had him on the satellite phone asking him if he could use his contacts to track The Rose of Tralee. He was a bit reluctant but after an acerbic exchange about duty and family he promised to get back to us.

By 1600 hours the satellite phone beeped and Catriona pulled it from its fitting. 'Angus?'

'Catriona. We think they are about 400 miles out into the Atlantic. A small trawler has been eyeballed from a commercial airliner turning onto a southerly course about that distance into the Atlantic. So you've got a bit of ground to make up. We'll update you every 24 hours as to their position.'

Catriona thanked him and cut the satellite connection. She relayed the information to me and we settled down for a stern chase. Like something out of Hornblower, I confided in her. She laughed and carried on making a watch list to divide the task of keeping the Mary Swift on course. I was given the daylight shift on the wheel while Catriona took the dark hours. Oh well, bang goes any chance of an erotic cuddle or two thought I. My next task was the cooking, and I was shooed off to the galley where I rustled up a very satisfactory fish chowder from a bit of frozen haddock and some prawns and a tin of sweetcorn all basted in a broth of milk and herbs and spices and thickened with some potatoes. Very nice. We sat and slurped it down with a slug or two of Bushmills. I retired to my cabin and fell asleep almost as soon as my head touched the pillow. Oblivious for the next eight hours or so I came awake to the regular sound of the 1000 hp Kelvin diesel engine powering us through the water. I luxuriously rose from my bunk, washed, dressed, and climbed the companionway to the wheelhouse.

Catriona was looking the worse for wear, though I wouldn't have told her so. Her eyes were red-rimmed and occasionally she stared off into the distance as if seeing demons dancing on the briny.

'Good morning my darling!' my bright greeting only received a grunt in return. Then she pulled herself together and explained our position and course and before I could complain she was off to her cabin to get some much-needed rest. I looked at the chart and the way master. We had come about 200 nautical miles overnight and were skirting the edge of the continental shelf off the republic of Ireland about 100 miles to the west. Once we left the shallow waters behind the Atlantic rollers could only come at us in bigger and bigger swells. However it was a fine day and a bunch of herring gulls were wheeling and calling around the stern of the boat. Fat chance for them. No fishing going on here mates. I set the autopilot and made a cup of much-needed coffee. Our course was straightforward, continuing out into the Atlantic until we were on the same latitude as Ushant, and then come due south; head on down through the Bay of Biscay and through the straits of Gibraltar. We'd needed to fuel up in Algeciras or Cueta before heading on for the coast of war-torn Libya.

Still no sign of the Arabs. Catriona's neat handwriting in the log registered a pretty non-eventful night. I hoped for the same during daylight hours. And so it transpired. Hour after hour the Mary Swift thrust her blunt nose into the green swell ahead of her and slowly I came to understand the different clocks and gauges that lined the wheelhouse walls. One of the most frightening was the depth gauge for fish finding. I pinged it on and a disembodied voice informed me that there were 400 fathoms of water below the hull and the sea bed. Shit Christ almighty, 2400 feet of nothing but cold green wet between me and Davy Jones's kingdom. I shivered.

About five o'clock a bleary eye and frowsty looking Catriona made it up to the wheelhouse. She cast an apprehensive eye around and when she realised that all was under control of the putative admiral in front of her, she skipped over and planted a huge wet kiss on my lips.

'Good boy Davie! We'll make a sailor of you yet! Anything to report?'

'Not a thing. Still no sign of the Libyans and we are about here.' I pointed to a spot on the chart, well out into the Atlantic by now.

She nodded. 'We could turn southerly anytime. Let's wait and see if Angus calls us and make our decision then.'

She'd hardly finished her sentence when the satellite phone pinged. Pulling the receiver to her she listened intently and grunted into it a few times. After the briefest of time she cut the connection and hung it back in its divits.

'Bloody MOD, they are refusing to help out with watching these Arab bastards in case it could be construed that extra help over and above the UN resolution was being used to finish this war.'

She stamped her well-formed foot. 'What a bunch of unmitigated wankers! I'd like to take one of Gadaffi's rockets and shove it up the arse of that twit in London.'

She shook her head in resignation and turned to the radar screen.

'Hey, what's this?'

I wandered over and gazed down on the computer's screen. Right on the very edge of the screen at the limits of the scan a green blip pulsed.

'Could be them. Could be anyone. Lets assume it's Al Arabi and pals and we'll follow after'.

She hit a few way points into the way master and rang up full ahead on the engine room telegraph. The Mary Swift gave a shudder as her big engine caught the excitement of full steam ahead, and she surged through the water with renewed vigour. Catriona was doing some calculations on her laptop and she sat back with a sigh of satisfaction.

'So if they are only 100 miles ahead of us and we can keep up 17 knots we'll be up with them in five or six hours. That'll bring us off the coast of Spain, and from there we can shadow them losing ourselves amongst the other marine traffic.'

'OK but what if we lose them?'

'Don't be so defeatist! It will be them, I feel it in my bones!'

For the next ten hours, as the sun sank into a cloudless sea and I garnered yet more sleep, Catriona followed the elusive green blip on the radar. When I surfaced next morning to find another balmy day in progress, the screen showed the coast of northern Spain off to the west, and our friend The Rose of Tralee steaming along much closer now. Before she went to her bed Catriona gave me explicit instructions.

'Don't get any closer than 25 miles to her. Keep out of her sight over the horizon, and if anything weird or unusual happens call me. Straight away!'

'Aye 'Aye captain.' I threw a mock salute and took over the wheel. Left alone in the wheelhouse I checked the log, our position on the chart and the green blip on the screen. All good, as far as I could tell. Ahead of me out on the briny, a pod of dolphins kept pace with the Mary Swift, gracefully leaping out of the water and then plunging back into it again. It was a game to them, and I thought back to an article I had read postulating that within five years we would be able to communicate with these wonderful marine creatures. Whether they would want to talk with us was another matter entirely.

Hours of monotonous steaming passed under our hull, and as the afternoon sun edged its way towards the horizon, Catriona appeared looking a hundred-percent better, having had a shower and washed her hair. Bright-eyed and bushy-tailed she kissed me and checked out the gauges and clocks.

'Fuel's getting a bit low; we may have to call into Lisbon or Cadiz. I don't think there's enough to get us into the Med.'

'No, we have been caning it a bit. Still, The Rose will have the same problem. I doubt she's fitted with long-range tanks. The radar showed a multitude of blips and it was difficult to pick out the one we thought might be the Arabs. We were within TV range off the coast, and the BBC news channel was still broadcasting the search for Gadaffi and the continuing battle for Tripoli and Sirte. Disquieting information and pictures of war crimes were filtering out from the war-torn capital and a sense of a new era in the fortunes of Libya came across the airwaves.

The radar blip we had been following so assiduously changed course abruptly and started to head due east towards the coast.

'Going for fuel, I'd say. We'll do the same'.

Our quarry headed in towards the land. It became obvious that she was heading for Lisbon. There was an extensive deep sea harbour and international port there and no difficulty in refuelling. We followed behind like a predatory cat stalking a mouse, always staying out of sight, never letting them know they were being followed. By midnight, The Rose of Tralee was berthed on a wooden jetty that ran crookedly down beside a stone wall that had edged the harbour for hundreds of years. We were likewise tied up but round the corner. Sure that the Arabs hadn't seen us, for the activity on board their boat was such that all of them were busy. A fuel line snaked into their fuel bunker, and once or twice, their patent leather shoes gleaming in the harsh light of the harbour floodlights, they came back to the boat carrying supplies. Around about four in the morning when most activity in the harbour had ceased, an old 1960's 190D Mercedes car with a taxi sign on the roof pulled up beside The Rose. Mohammed Al Arabi and his two goons got in, leaving at least three others still working on deck.

Catriona and I decided to follow them as best we could. As a precaution, we each fetched a Walther PPK from the arms chest and climbed on to one of the wooden trolley cars that ply their trade through the steep streets of Lisbon. Built by British engineers at the turn of the century and lovingly maintained ever since by the Portuguese. This city transit trolley car system is ideal for the steep and narrow streets of the old town. In fact it is a darn sight easier and quicker that trying it by car. For a lack of parking etiquette and the sheer number of cars parked on the streets meant that most often the roadways were blocked by stationary traffic, all except the steel rails that snaked up the hill towards Al Fama. Our trolley, a lovingly maintained work of art in varnished wood and curved glass with leather-upholstered seats, was almost empty. Some early workers on their way to a days' toil shared it with us. Up ahead I glimpsed the rounded shape of the pontoon merc. Lisbon is a city with more old cars still in service than anywhere else in the world with the exception of Havana. Chevrolets from the Fifties, Fords from the Thirties and Mercs, Mercs, Mercs from every era. Some quite rare that would have fetched a premium price in Germany or the UK had they ever been exported. Occasionally a down-at-mouth horse pulling a tourist carriage would clop past. Our trolley clanked and banged as it swung its way up the cobbled streets. Ahead brake lights gleamed, and the 190 pulled into the side. The three Arabs got out and started to walk down a narrow lane that led into the heart of the Al Fama.

This was a district renowned for its small restaurants and bars and for the high levels of street crime, and a centre for organised crime in the city. A myriad of tiny cobbled alleyways and streets, often too narrow to walk two abreast, snaked their way across the steep hill that made up most of the Al Fama District. We got off the trolley bus and plunged into the foetid smelling alleyways. The sound of Fado: that plaintiff sad music that haunts the bars of Lisbon, came from a lit doorway ahead. I glimpsed the heel of a patent leather shoe disappear inside, and pulling Catriona by the arm, we followed. A fug of smoke greeted us. At one end, almost indistinct because of the tobacco smoke, a small raised dais upon which a beautiful middle-aged singer with silver grey in her hair was wailing out a fado tune, whilst her guitarist was giving his all to the complicated rhythm. Sitting with their backs to us and some way into the crowded room were the three we had been following. I sank down onto an unoccupied chair well away from their line of sight. Catriona followed my lead. The Arabs were listening attentively to another individual who was dressed in a very expensive silk three-piece suit. Every so often he pulled a silk handkerchief from his breast pocket and mopped his sweating brow. Beside him sat another swarthy looking man, not an Arab but of some indeterminate middle European race, Bulgarian, Hungarian or Slav body guard, I thought. Every so often this individual would scan across the room with his cold little eyes. A frightening sight if they fell on you for any length of time. Luckily he didn't know us from Adam, but Al Arabi and his goons did. However they kept their eyes and attention on the silk-suited one. The fado song wound its way towards its sad conclusion, and a smattering of polite applause encouraged the singer to start again. A waiter appeared and we ordered a beer apiece. The table ahead of us, and partially obscuring our sight of the Arabs, suddenly became empty. Catriona turned away in horror as Al Arabi turned and glanced back in her direction. An angry look of recognition flashed across his face, and he shouted something to one of his companions. Instantly all hell broke loose. Reaching into his coat pocket the goon pulled out a plastic glock pistol and shot off two rounds in our direction. Luckily, both missed, but one round shattered the beer bottles that our waiter was bringing us showering him and a woman in a low-cut dress with broken glass and beer foam. Screams of horror and male shouts of indignation welled up within the room. Another two pistol shots echoed into the room of a different, deeper, note and I realised that Catriona had pulled out her Walther and was returning fire. One of the Arabs spun away wounded and the Slav bodyguard had slumped to the floor.

'Out of here,' I screamed, and we fled. In the confusion we were able to disappear into one of the dark alleyways that run to and fro throughout the Al Fama, and by the time we could hear the sound of police sirens making their way to the Fado bar we had safely run down the steep hill towards the harbour, and were back on board the Mary Swift. Our first task was to refuel, and although it was only six o'clock in the morning, an unusual bustle of activity was taking place about the harbour. We were able to fill our tanks, pay and cast off our mooring lines, all before The Rose of Tralee was fully awake. We steamed out to sea passing the monument to Christopher Columbus that stands majestically at the start of the harbour.

The Mary Swift was making good progress. We had just passed the entrance to the enclosed water that makes up the harbour area, and were heading out into the open sea. We were congratulating ourselves on having escaped from the murderous Arabs when from behind us in the misty, early morning light, through the polluted grey swathe of Lisbon's harbour I saw a long, sleek, low-lying, blue and white boat come tearing towards us. The wheelhouse was painted with the one word, Policia.

'Shit!' I cried, 'Police boat on our right.'

Catriona took a look. 'We'll never outrun that. We'd better heave to and face the music.'

She eased the throttle back, and the Mary Swift dropped down onto her bow wave and slowly came to a stop in the water. The police boat came alongside, and two tough looking men dressed in dark navy clothes with sub-machine guns slung about them climbed over the gunwale and on to the deck. Following them came another man. This one dressed in a tight fitting uniform with much insignia upon it and his peaked hat covered with scrambled egg. His epaulettes stood out like boards from his shoulders and he wore mirror aviator shades that hid his eyes. A pistol in an unbuttoned holster lay at his side and a very flashy Brietling wristwatch adorned his wrist. He also climbed aboard, looked around and pulled off his glasses. I nearly fainted, for the last time I had seen him had been in the Fado bar talking so animatedly with the Arabs. He smiled: the smile of a snake, and shook his head in mock sadness.

'Now, you come with us!' he ordered, and his two henchmen unslung their weapons and pointed them uncompromisingly in our direction. They marched us to the side, and with a prod of their guns forced us down on to the deck of the police boat. Mr Big followed with a swagger one sees only amongst the upper echelons of authority in foreign parts where power and authority emanate from the barrel of a gun. This was Portugal, for God's sake; a member of the European Union, not Libya or Tunisia or Syria. One of the policemen stayed behind to con the Mary Swift back to harbour, and we pulled away in a flurry of bow wave with our siren blaring and the LCD lights across the top of the wheelhouse flashing in unison like a demented clown show.

We were manhandled none-to-lightly into a grim little grey office that stank of sweat and old tobacco smoke.

'Sit!' We obeyed. Mr Big removed his silly hat and smoothed his hand through the bay rum smelling grease that plastered his black-dyed hair to his head.

'So, you think you can shoot at the chief of Police and not suffer the consequences?'

'Chief of Police? Shit, I thought you were part of an organised crime gang.'

He smiled that snake smile again.

'That also. But now I am Police.' Here his voice took on a harsh hectoring tone that didn't bode well for the pair of us. 'My friends tell me you are thorns in the side, that each time he sees you, things go wrong for him.'

I smiled smugly. Instantly he was out of his chair and he slapped me hard across the face with his leather-gloved hand. 'Shut up boy, you don't know what trouble you are in!'

My bowels turned to water and I was in danger of shitting my pants. Only by a supreme effort of will was I able to clench my sphincter and avoid a humiliation.

'This is what happens now.' His voice dropped to a smooth almost whispering cadence as he proceeded to lay out the choice for us that he had conceived.

'We take you out into the mountains where no one will miss you and no one will find you, and we kill you. OK?'

His matter-of-fact tone chilled me. I felt a terrible loss of hope and cold, unmitigated fear washed over me. Catriona sat slumped before him with a look of horror on her face. He snapped his fingers and a muscled looking cop came in.

'Take these two to the Casa del Romero, and deal with them.'

The man grinned and pulling his pistol from its holster he ordered us out of the room. Forcing us at gunpoint down into a basement garage we got into an unmarked and battered Seat car.

'You drive,' he shouted at Catriona.

'Sorry pal, can't drive, don't know how,' came her reply.

Next he tried me; I gave the same reply. He pulled his mobile from his uniform jacket pocket and a fast and voluble conversation took place. Within a few minutes another policeman arrived and this one slid in behind the wheel and started the engine. Number-one cop forced us into the back seat and took up position in the front with his gun pointed at us. A hopeless situation to be in. I turned my head towards Catriona and in the broadest Scottish accent I could manage, so as to confuse the cops, I said, 'Welly the back of the seats when I shout!'

The cop driving let in the clutch and with a squeal the battered old Seat surged forward. We took a road out of Lisbon into the interior clattering and banging along the dusty road. Although this was an unmarked police car there was very little evidence that it was maintained and in fact I could see that the front seats were only fixed to the floor by thin brackets. I hoped my plan would work. Assuming we were heading towards Armageddon, we had nothing to lose. The driver floored the accelerator and the car screamed as it pulled up a steep incline. He swung off the main road onto an unmarked and unmettalled minor road. There was no diminution in speed and the suspension banged and groaned as the little car was subjected to the worst Portuguese roads could throw at it. The two cops were holding a conversation. The one with the gun had lowered his weapon and was looking forward. The road took a hard turn to the left and then started to drop down through a series of blind hairpin bends. The treed vegetation came right down to the road edge on one side and then dropped steeply away on the other with just a few thin saplings to stop a vehicle plunging hundreds of feet down to a rocky, silver mountain stream in the valley below.

I screamed out, 'Welly the seats,' and together and without warning we both kicked hard and I mean hard, once, twice, three times. Cop one, with the gun, was catapulted forward against the windscreen and fell back unconscious with a trickle of blood coming from his head. The driver totally lost control of his vehicle, and the next minute we were careening over the edge of the road. Luckily there was a fairly substantial young ash tree edging the roadside and the Seat crashed into that. The driver shot forward and banged his head with a nasty cracking crunch that didn't bode well for any future neck-aches. The car stopped, steam pouring from the bonnet.

'Are you all right?' I cried in alarm.

Catriona grinned, 'Couldn't be better. Let's deal with these bastards!'

We eased open the doors and pulled the two policemen out onto the road. The driver was dead: his neck broken and his head at an odd angle. Cop two was still unconscious. We rummaged through the glove compartment and found a roll of silver gaffer tape. I bound his ankles and wrists and slapped a couple of strips across his mouth. Then, trussed like a chicken, I threw the bastard down against the trunk of a tree and started to undress him. Catriona was dealing in the same manner with the other. We removed their outer clothes, baseball caps and mirror sunglasses. Their radios and pistols and anything else that was useful. Then we dressed ourselves in their uniforms. Nothing was said between us, it was if we were operating to some scenario already agreed.

Stepping back from the still-steaming car I looked at my companion. Her uniform was slightly too big for her, but for all intents and purposes she was a loyal member of the Policia Judicia a Lisboa. She pulled on the mirror shades to complete the disguise. 'We should be able to get back to the boat like this and get the hell out of here.' She hefted the gun. 'Tidy little weapon. Add it into our armoury!'

I lifted the crunched bonnet of the Seat. I was worried that all the steam coming out from under meant that the radiator was damaged. I needn't have worried. In the crash the filler cap had been twisted off and only about half the water in the rad. had been lost. There was a bottle of water in the car and we used that to top up. Then Catriona got behind the wheel and reversed out of the tree-lined road edge. There was a nasty grinding and clanking but it was only the left-hand wing bent forward over the wheel and I soon fixed that with a savage kick or two. Before we left I threw the dead body of the policeman down the ravine and his companion after him. Sod it; those bastards would have done worse to us. I climbed aboard and we set off at a sedate pace back the way we had come.

KILLER ISLAND

Chapter Nine

Within an hour we were driving back through the harbour gates and down to the wharf where we could see the Mary Swift tied up next to the fast patrol boat of the Police. There was no one in sight. It was midday and the bastards were having a siesta. All to the good. We pulled up and got out of the car. A fiendish plan popped into my head. I told Catriona, and she laughed. She climbed aboard the Mary Swift and started her up. Meanwhile I backed the Seat away from the wharf and lined it up for its final journey. Engaging second gear and revving the engine, I set the little Spanish car on its way over the quay edge and crashing down onto the fast patrol boat below. There was a cacophony of tortured metal shrieks as the one-and-a-half ton car fell three metres onto the marine ply deck of the motor boat. A gurgling sound instantly started from below and before I had time to unmoor the Mary Swift and climb aboard, the police boat was down by the head with the little car sitting incongruously on its deck. We backed the Mary Swift out of the harbour and by the time we had passed the Columbus monument there was no sign of the car or the police boat.

I laughed. 'That'll teach the pricks. Don't tangle with Scottish lads and lassies.'

Catriona laughed out loud. 'Well Davie, my love, being a member of MI6 has certainly brought out the macho in you ,'and she planted a huge kiss on my lips. I swaggered like a cockerel; I almost crowed. Then I looked ahead. A rolling bank of mist thicker than grey cream was barrelling in towards us.

'Shit, we'll never make our way in that.'

'Don't worry, it's to our advantage; it'll hide us from prying eyes and we'll use the satnav to get through it. Come on, take the wheel. I'll plot a course.'

Holding the engine revs low, we sank into the mist and the clammy cold closed around us. Visibility dropped to less than a metre and I flicked on the fog horn. From all sides the eerie disembodied sound of fog horns of all types sounded out like the last laments of the sirens that had lured Odysseus to his fate. But he never had radar and we did. We were able to thread our way through the other craft on the water, and as the sound of fog horns slowly started to fall away behind us we suddenly came out of the fog bank into blazing sunlight. Not a ship in sight. We seemed to be the only marine inhabitants anywhere around the horizon, and calling for full ahead, I turned the Mary Swift onto a course for Gibraltar and the Hellespont.

Approximately 1500 miles to the straits of Gibraltar, and we didn't see another boat. The weather remained calm, and we made good progress keeping the engine room telegraph on full ahead. The little blips on the radar were all within the med. God knows where The Rose of Tralee had got too. She could have been anyone of those tiny little green ovals around which the radar scanner swept. Without a definitive sighting it was like choosing one chick pea from another. Two days and a night after we escaped the clutches of the Portuguese police, we came in sight of the fabled Hellespont of ancient times. We hadn't been apprehended by any strange cops, shot at by North Africans, or generally subjected to the miscellany of adventures that had dogged us since we discovered the toxic waste on the Island. Our fuel was low and so were supplies and we decided to call at the rock and do some shopping. Being a British protectorate we hoped we might be able to gain some information as to the whereabouts of Al Arabi and his friends. I knew from previous research that Gibraltar was a hub for the gathering and dissemination of intelligence appertaining to the Mediterranean area.

We pulled into the harbour. Several warships, a class two frigate, and an aircraft carrier were moored in the roads. This looked like the whole extent of the Royal Navy moored here in front of us. Then I realised that only the class two frigate was ours. A limp red ensign drooping from the flagpole in the still airs. The other boats were from Russia, the US and France. Further in, and closer to the Rock itself, were moored two large sail training vessels. Boats from another era with three masts each and a myriad spiders web of rigging running up their bare poles. Smart navy cadets from Norway and Lithuania were having a party on the deck of one of the boats as we slowly moved past in the direction of our berth. A very pretty girl dressed in a smart blue and white uniform raised her arm in greeting and smiled. The sun shone down and the granite bastion of British naval achievement glowered in its place off the coast of Spain.

We tied up in the spot designated by customs, and an over-officious officer and his assistant descended on us and gave us a cursory search. We had dumped the police uniforms some miles back, and they were unable to find our stash of weapons hidden as they were in a specially constructed hole in the sole of the wheelhouse. Given a clean bill of health we disembarked, and Catriona went off to find fuel and I took a taxi into town to the nearest supermarket.

An hour later an £100 lighter in the credit card, I returned with many plastic bags of provisions to find a fuel line snaking down over the deck and filling our bunker with much-needed fuel. Catriona was sitting on a bollard on the wharf with a mobile phone to her ear. Seeing me, she cut the connection and said,'That was the Laird. I've just fixed to see Commander Richards of Nav Intell. Tomorrow at 9 a.m in his office in High Town.I hope he'll have some facts for us. The Laird was none too pleased with our ding-dong with the Portuguese cops, but he thinks he can smooth it out.'

I looked doubtful. 'There's not a lot of smoothing needs doing with that criminal. Straight to Jail. Do not pass go etc etc I should think.'

'Aye you're right. I shudder when I think about the callous way he said he was just going to kill us!'

'Well, we've nearly filled up the fuel. MI6 is taking care of the bill and the Laird's given us the go ahead to keep chasing Al Arabi. It's over a thousand miles to Tripoli from here, so I think we should get on with it.'

'Good idea, Captain.'

I threw a mock salute. 'But not before the morning, eh?'

Chapter Ten

By nine o'clock next morning the two of us were walking up the road to High Town. It was a wonderful, sparkling fresh morning with a distant view of the African mainland off to the right, whilst right behind us the mainland of Europe and its tapas- eating inhabitants gleamed in the new day. We were looking for the offices of Naval Intelligence and specifically Commander Richards. Ahead of us, an armed naval rating in white top and knee breeches, stood guard over the entrance to a baroque building that wouldn't have disgraced Horse Guards. Ascertaining that this was indeed Nav Intell we entered the air conditioned great hall, and the middle-aged sergeant receptionist phoned our details up to the third floor. In due course, we entered the offices of Commander Richards, who turned out to be a charming thirty something woman with her hair tied back in a chignon and wearing a light tropical navel uniform.

'OK. I've got various stuff for you. I hope it's useful.' She spun a computer screen round on her desk and a screen showed a page of information. We leant forward to read it. The Rose of Tralee had made port in Cueta the day before. There was an attached satellite photo taken from five miles up, but enhanced to show the Arab goons

75

sunning themselves on the deck as a fuel line filled their diesel tank.

Commander Richards reached into her desk and pulled out a sheaf of flimsy pink papers.

'Most of this arrived from the UK this morning and I think you need to read it.'

She passed the papers across to Catriona who started to read them.

'Shit almighty: they don't want much do they.' She passed the papers over to me.

The first was headed "Top Secret MI6 for authorised eyes only" and the contents were a list of instructions. For us: for little old temporary MI6 operatives, Catriona and Davie.

No 1: Shadow and keep surveillance on the trawler Rose of Tralee.

No2. Once cargo is off-loaded to mainland Libya, wherever that might be, to follow cargo to its destination.

No3. Destroy and disable cargo. Likewise any hostile operatives.

'Well, fucking Christ, they don't want much. I'm not doing it!'

Commander Richards smiled. 'Sorry Davie, but I'm afraid you have to. You signed some papers back in the UK?'

I nodded and my heart sank; I knew what carrot and stick was dangling over my donkey nose.

'If you don't obey these MI6 instructions you're in contravention of your contract with them and you'd both end up in Belmarsh. Twenty-five years, minimum, for treason!'

That such a charming woman with such a sweet-smelling persona could have a heart of unrefined steel like this quite shocked me.

She went on, 'Read this one. I think it'll make things easier for you.'

She passed over another flimsy. This one had a list of personnel on it. Three of them Sergeant Gilbraith, Corporal Smith and Trooper Bathurst all from SAS Special Unit Hereford; all trained in the dark arts of infiltration into enemy territory and to kill silently whilst still being able to operate a computer under stress, and charm diplomatic missions in far-flung parts of the world. In fact, one of those non-attributable units that the government emphatically denied was on the ground in Libya helping the rebels. If you took all the deniable units out of the equation from France, Italy, Quatar and anyone else who'd tried to help, the rebels would never have made the gains they had. That and the unrelenting air strikes by NATO had swung the war firmly into the hands of the Transitional Council. However, there still seemed a long way to go before the Libyans were truly liberated, and a new democracy was born in the country.

'You're to pick-up with these guys once you get into Libya. They'll disguise you and arm you and help you destroy these bastards.'

Commander Richards' use of language had me smiling. Charming woman, with her heart of steel and her Chanel No 5.

'Last one,' she passed across a flimsy with a list of the ICBMs and other military weapons Gaddafi was likely to have. It was an extensive list, starting with truck- launched Grad missiles which we'd all see pics of through scuds developed by the Soviets in the 80's, and ending with the big ones capable of delivering chemical warheads: Shehabs

4,5 and 6 probably acquired form the Iranians. These were not too much of a threat being notoriously inaccurate and unreliable, though the Shehab 4 had a range of 200 km. Quite enough to strike anywhere in the country.

More damaging and worrying were the ICBM s: the Redong 1. Developed from an earlier scud design by N Korea and capable of a 1500 mile range with a warhead which detached after 110 seconds of motor power and came back into the atmosphere using its own guidance system. This was dangerous! Were these the boys Gadaffi had it in mind to arm with anthrax spores and toxic waste? One of those set off towards Europe without even a destination fixed in its guidance system, and the whole balance of power could be altered for years to come. Not only that, but the extravagant loss of innocent civilian life made me shudder.

'So, what are MI6 expecting us to do then?' I asked with an almost plaintiff tone to my voice, some would say a whine. Commander Richards looked at me.

'Oh, destroy the toxic materials, kill the Arabs, destroy all the ICBMs and generally clean up after yourselves.'

'What, me and Catriona and three squaddies? Fat chance, and we're not even getting paid!'

'Oh, there'll most probably be a gong in it for you, even if it is posthumous.'

'Bloody dinner gong most like,' I sniffed.

Catriona added her three pence worth. 'Come on Davie, we've come this far, let's look on it as an adventure holiday!'

'Oh aye, visit the beautiful countryside of Libya, get attacked by grad rockets and shot at by nutter-Gadaffi loyalists. Stay in ruined hotels with no drinking water and even as a thrilling bonus, end up dead!'

The fax machine on Commander Richards' desk started to bleep and out of its maw spewed a piece of paper. I glanced across. It was a satellite pic of The Rose of Tralee leaving port. A slew of printing followed after: '*The Rose of Tralee with five personnel and the captain on board exited port 0900 hours today. Several crates contents unknown were loaded onto the boat and several tubular containers. Contents unknown*'. The fax machine clattered to a finish.

'OK,' I said 'We better get back after them, can't afford to give them too much of a lead. If any more up-to-date intel comes in send it to us on the boat.'

The commander nodded in the affirmative, and we left and walked back down the hill from High Town and to the berth where the Mary Swift was tied up.

Our boat had been fully provisioned in our absence right down to a couple of bottles of Bushmills. All courtesy of MI6. They weren't prepared to pay us but they were prepared to equip us with the best in drinking liquor. Thanks MI6, nice one.

We cast off and headed out into the busy sea lanes around the rock. It was a lovely quiet day. Just a few small pleasure yachts criss-crossing the harbour with their pristine white sails and spinnakers aloft. One of the sail training boats was readying for sea with the cadets out on the yardarms waiting for the order to unfurl. A fast cigarette boat creating a giant bow wave sped by at what looked like thirty knots across the limit of my vision as I stared out at the coast of Africa. The Ferry from Algerciras to Cueta blew its foghorn in a joyful expression of good will, and we left the rock behind.

It was more than a thousand miles to the coast of Libya, at least to Tripoli. Although it was a safe bet to assume the enemy wouldn't be unloading there! But maybe at Sirte. Still, a Gaddafi loyalist stronghold, and at this moment in time there was no fighting there as the rebels waited for an ultimatum to expire before they released their considerable fire power in what they hoped would be the last battle of the war. The more I thought about it the more of a Fred Karno moment it became. Still some idiot had to do it and that idiot was me; admirably backed up by the beautiful green-eyed Catriona.

The radar showed the ubiquitous green oval that was The Rose, tracking along the coast of North Africa, keeping snug into the land as if slightly embarrassed to move out into deeper water. We parallel-tracked her, always keeping her about fifty miles away; within radar sight but out of vision below the horizon. After a day and a night of following with no discernable difference to either vessel, we were bored and hot. A gritty wind had started up, blowing in a red dust that settled on everything, but we were closer to our destination by a couple of hundred miles. The only place to get much relief from the horrid dust of the offshore wind was down in the air conditioned cabins. So we each took it in turn to have time off on our bunks. I spent it asleep on the assumption that a sleep debt paid off would benefit me in the future, especially if there was going to be a lot of frightening gun action on the mainland. I assumed Catriona did the same, as there were only the two of us to sail the Mary Swift, there was very little time to indulge in hanky panky of the sexual variety. I did need some loving but it wasn't appropriate so I had to limit myself to the occasional snog grabbed at the turnover of duties when I took over the tiller, or got banished into the galley. I must say, my culinary skills were shaping up, and as I cooked kidney beans and harries in a tomato sauce, or fried up fresh fish caught over the side that morning, my mind turned on the idea of writing a cookery book of recipes for the discerning war correspondent. Catriona's input was, 'OK bomb surprise would be good,' and she laughed in a particular way. Still, her beans on toast with sliced gherkins put a new dimension on the term fast food. Ready in thirty seconds thanks to the microwave, and a very tasty meal indeed!

So we schlepped through the less than murky waters off the North African coast. By day three out of Gib., we were coming closer to the coast of Libya. The green edge of Tunisia slid by on our right though out of sight. The island of Malta, was to our left, but also out of sight. We intercepted some radio messages for us, in a sort of schoolboy code that the meanest intelligence ought to have been able to decipher, to the effect that our SAS team was waiting for us. They didn't say where. I hoped somewhere like Sirte, but knowing the chaos that was going on in the interior it could be anywhere. We read the messages, shrugged and kept going. As the coast of Tunisia ran out and the coast of Libya slid into view a feeling of anxiety and dread started to build in my mind. I cleaned all the weapons and checked out the ammo and grenades; feeling slightly more macho as a result. I was calculating a course along the coast to Sirte when Catriona called over.

'Hey Davie, it looks like The Rose has changed course.'

I Walked over to the radar to confirm that The Rose had indeed swung off her original course and was heading towards the coast.. It looked like a Tripoli landfall.

'I think they're going to pass themselves off as rebels and spirit their cargo into the interior. Why else head for Tripoli? It's in Rebel hands and any fighting has long finished there.

'Yes, better than Sirte, that's surrounded by rebels, and I doubt a mouse could leave from any road there!'

'You're so right. I wonder if our SAS team know about this? I'll give Nav intell a bell.'

She grabbed the radio phone and scarfed herself into the network. Within minutes she was having an animated conversation with Commander Richards. After a few moments of mutual smiling and bonhomie she replaced the receiver.

'Good woman that, must introduce her to the Laird. So, she says they're tracking The Rose's every move, and the SAS are getting ready to meet us as soon as we dock.'

I looked again at the radar. The Rose had swung into the coast and was in danger of being consumed by the lights from the city. We were still some fifty miles or so off the coast but our heading mirrored that of The Rose. We steamed steadily towards the ravaged land that had suffered so terribly under the mad dog dictator Gaddafi for forty-two years, and had then suffered a modern killing destructive war for six months.

Chapter Eleven

Deep in the Libyan desert surrounded by nothing but orange and yellow sandstone bluffs, low hills and sand dunes where only one tarmac road ran in a sand blown, oven- heated hell on its way to the border with Chad some hundreds of kilometres south, stood the last loyalist stronghold of Shaba. It had grown up over the years as a result of Gaddafi's mad idea of building the definitive airfield and WMD faculty. The airfield once housed a wing of Mig 25 fighter bombers amounting to about fifty planes, and away from the airfield, in reinforced concrete bunkers built into the sand stone bluffs that surround it, was a state-of-the-art laboratory and research centre where chemical weapons were developed and a burgeoning nuclear warhead facility was centered. In deep silos scattered around this area were kept all the mad dictator's stock of ICBMs. These included a dozen Redong 1 and Shehab 4,5 and 6s. It did not include the huge stock of Grad rockets on their launchers, which were neatly parked in the reinforced concrete hangers built deep into the rock of the sandstone bluffs. Or the scud missiles which Gaddafi had taken to firing indiscriminately at his civilian population. Although the 'Great Leader' had forsworn WMDs back in the eighties and had gone some way to showing the West that he had destroyed many of his capabilities, there was always a tricky side to the man, and playing off one end against the other he had kept the Shaba facility and sunk millions and millions of Libyan Dinars into it.

About a thousand loyal troops, including his much-vaunted female battalion, were here. His son, the feared Shami who was the commander of the Shalamis' Brigade known for the ruthless rape and indiscriminate killing of its victims, was also in residence. They were waiting for Gaddafi, who was believed to still be in Beni Walid. But that was three-hundred miles away and could be a difficult journey with the rebels controlling most of the tarmacked roads.

In an air conditioned laboratory a team of scientists were putting together a toxic chemical warhead capable of being delivered by the scuds outside. They were waiting the arrival of some added ingredients they had been promised from Europe and at this moment the work had come to an end. They were discussing the state of the war.

'The rats and dogs in Tripoli will never win; they will be wiped from the land by the righteous wrath of our great leader Mohammed Gaddafi,' shouted out one of the scientists, repeating the rhetoric he had heard on the audio broadcasts coming from Syrian Radio. It had been many weeks since Gaddafi had broadcast in person on the television. Without knowing his whereabouts for certain, the only contact his loyal subjects had was with the almost nightly rant that came from the radio.

'He has said we must fight a guerrilla war; we must burn the ground under them and women and children must come out of their houses and fight in the alleyways.' One white-coated scientist shook his clenched fist in anger and spat. 'Death to all traitors of Libya!'

Another white-coated technician confidentially said, 'He will come south down the Great Man-Made River and once he is here, we'll have a victory to outshine all other victories.' The other scientists clapped and cheered and waved photos of their leader. An army officer held his hands up. 'Silence my brothers. It is time to start the great work again. Back to your desks. Redouble your efforts for the better good of Libya. With renewed vigour, the scientists returned to their tasks and a concentrated hum of activity settled over the laboratory.

Outside on the huge tarmacked parade ground, a team of fifty or so uniformed troops with fore-end loaders were starting to erect the gantries for the Redong rockets. NATO had already bombed this facility but had only taken out the airfield. The rocket launching area was untouched. In a deep underground silo the Redongs were being checked over. Was their propellant still active; were the warhead guidance systems still functioning properly? These rockets could fly for 1500 kilometres with a motor thrust time of 110 secs which took them out of the earth's atmosphere. Then the motor cut out and the warhead detached itself and using its own guidance system it re-entered the atmosphere and hopefully fell on its designated target. However none of these had ever been fired in anger, and of the test rockets that had been fired only about a third had been successful.

The scuds on the other hand were only too good. Developed by the Soviets for use in tactical theatres like Afghanistan, they had proved their worth as tank busters and copter killers time and time again. They were capable of a 200 km. range and were often shoulder-launched. The final nasty in the armoury were the Grads. Mounted on the back of 10 ton Zil lorries in banks of forty at a time, these fearsome weapons were quickly and easily deployed around any war theatre. With a two minute reload time they could be fired, driven to safety, and be ready to go again before the shocked recipient realised he was under attack. Their greatest disadvantage was their appalling inaccuracy. Many times military targets had been completely missed and collateral damage to civilian sites nearby had been enormous!

Out in the desert in the 40 degrees plus of the Libyan summer, only the hardiest camel and goat could survive. The locals, mainly Bedouin, from which Gaddafi claimed descent, though this could have been a marketing ploy to make his persona more appealing to the West, had existed here for hundreds of years. Leading a nomadic life, herding their flocks across the inhospitable terrain and generally not bothering any one. In 1986 a huge new infrastructure project started up. Nothing less than to bring unlimited sweet drinking water to the inhabitants of Libya who were mainly living along the coastal strip from Tripoli to Benghasi. Huge reserves of aquifer water had been discovered in deep reservoirs under the desert laid down millennia ago when the sea reached inland past the mountains. The project required hundreds of kilometres of huge reinforced concrete pipes, eight metres in diameter, to be buried seven metres down in the desert, sealed and pressure tested. Thousands of Libyans worked on the project, and the network of pipes stretched across the country bringing life: giving water to all populous regions and allowing agriculture to thrive. It cost in excess of 25 bn US dollars and royally pissed off the yanks who didn't believe such a huge project could be undertaken without their money and input. However, they were proved wrong, and in due course of time the water flowed and the people drank.

In his mad-dog way, however, Gaddafi had decided to cut off the water to his subjects, and the Great Man-Made River ran dry and also became an ideal bolt hole and escape tunnel for him to arrive in Shaba.

Chapter Twelve

According to our radar, The Rose of Tralee had berthed in Tripoli harbour. The oval blip was stationary, tied up against the wharf in one of the most run down parts of the harbour. We rang up full ahead, and steamed in after them. Having kept away by fifty miles or so in order not to be seen, there was always the possibility that they'd off- load their cargo and disappear into the interior before we got into harbour. As we came round the mole into the large and surprisingly empty harbour area, a fast Libyan patrol boat swung away from the wharf and made its way towards us. The rebel flag was flying from a stubby radio mast, and there were at least six tough looking men in army fatigue camo trousers and green short-sleeved tee-shirts, with their heads covered from the sun by baseball caps or Arabic scarves; in fact a typical rebel cohort. Their boat swung up alongside and a voice in English hailed us.

'Ho! Mary Swift. We've come to assist you. Can we come aboard?'

'Are you Sergt. Galbraith and friends?' I hollered back.

He nodded in the affirmative, and moments later three Arabic-looking men had climbed over the tumblehome on to the deck of the Mary Swift. The tallest and most swarthy shook my hand.

'Jimmy Gilbraith, at your service. I'm in charge of this bunch of heathens, but I've been told to defer to you two if necessary.'

I felt a warm glow of something akin to pride as I gazed at the trio. Each man would not have been noticed had they been thrown down in any souk in North Africa. Each and every one looked as Arabic or Libyan as you could hope for, right down to the extravagant moustaches and three-days growth of beards that graced their smiling faces.

'This is Corp. Smith, SAS hard man; looks like this cos his mum is Algerian, speaks two or three native languages and is fluent in Libyan.'

The man grinned and stuck out his hand.

'Pleased to meet you sir and madam,' he said in a broad Geordie accent.

I took an instant liking to his looks and gruff manner.

'This rebel rat is trooper Bathhurst. Double first in Arabic studies at Cambridge; a better man in a fight it would be hard to find.'

The man inclined his head and smiled broadly.

Gilbraith continued, 'We better try and disguise you both a bit, cos at the moment you look like press corp refugees, and that'll never do. Come into the wheelhouse and we'll see what we can do.'

He picked up a leather case and carried it down the companionway and clicked it open on the table. Inside were several bottles of a walnut-coloured dye and other make-up items which he proceeded to apply to our faces, arms and hands, and not forgetting the exposed ankles. Catriona was transformed. From being a red-haired, green-eyed, pale-skinned Celtic beauty, Gilbraith transformed her into a sultry red- haired, green-eyed North African beauty, complete with nose ring. He passed her a djellaba to wear. He slapped the walnut dye on my face and darkened my hair down several shades, and equipped me with the ubiquitous rebel uniform of camo trousers and tee-shirt.

Passing me a hand mirror he said, 'I defy anyone out there to mistake Khalid and Ayesha from the genuine article.'

Looking in the mirror I thought: By Christ, or Mohammed, he's right. A swarthy looking dark-skinned, slightly suspect Arab stared back at me. Even when I smiled the look of the souk gleamed back at me.

'Weapons, Davie, Sir. You can have this automatic machine pistol.' He passed me a fearsome looking teak-handled gun, which he proceeded to demonstrate.

'Catriona, Ma'am, would you care for this slightly lighter version which you could wear under your djellaba?'

She laughed, 'No discrimination then Serge. What I really want, what I really really want is a sharp dagger and some hand grenades. Got any of those?'

He laughed out loud and passed over both items. She strapped the dagger to her side, and hefted the gun and tossed the leather satchel of grenades over her shoulder.

'Well now, boys, lead on. I'm ready for war,' and she gave a little swagger.

'Any other weapons for you Davie Sir?' I shook my head.

'No this gun is fine, and leave out the sir will you. Davie's quite good enough thank you!'

'That goes for me too Sarge, my name's Catriona and that's what I'll answer too OK?'

The sergeant grinned. 'OK by me: Catriona and Davie it is. I'm Jim, he's Khali,' pointing at Corporal Smith, 'and he's Aiden,' pointing at Trooper Bathhurst. 'OK let's go and find these bastards and see what they're up to.'

They disembarked from the Mary Swift and walked across the quay side until they came to a battered white Toyota pick-up truck with a 35mm automatic machine gun mounted in the truck bed. This vehicle looked liked the ubiquitous rebel truck complete with rebel flag. Aiden and Khali climbed in the back and Catriona and Davie got into the cab. Jim behind the wheel. He fired up the engine and immediately it was obvious that this was no ordinary Toyota. The engine note was deeper and more powerful and the transmission was permanent four-wheel drive. The bodywork however was just as dusty and overwritten with Arabic script as any of the other hundreds of such vehicles that the rebels used. Gilbraith swung the vehicle towards the other end of the harbour and they roared over towards the part where The Rose of Tralee was docked. The trawler was there all right, but of its occupants there was no sign. They climbed on board but the vessel was deserted. The hold was empty and there was no sign of any occupants. Some dock workers wandered over and the Sergeant engaged them in conversation. It transpired that as soon as The Rose had docked, a ten-ton lorry and a forklift had swung by the trawler and proceeded to offload the cargo. As soon as it was done, the lorry and the men from the trawler had departed out the gates. The worker in his once-white boiler suit gesticulating towards the northern exit.

'Shit and bollocks, we've just missed them. They can't have got far; we'll take the road to the interior. I bet that's their direction.'

He climbed back into the Toyota and gunned the engine. They raced out of the harbour gates and joined the ever-increasing traffic on the main road that ran round Tripoli Harbour. Eventually this gave way to directions in Arabic for the interior and the road north to Tunis. Taking the road for the interior, Gilbraith floored the accelerator and the pick-up responded like the thoroughbred she was. Some parts of the city had been badly mauled in the fighting, with blackened buildings and walls with shell holes in them. Rubble still littered the streets, but the inhabitants were slowly getting back to some semblance of normality. Shops were open, men were sitting at roadside cafes, and the traffic was increasing. As they drove past the outer residential areas where jerry built high-rise blocks marred the skyline, they started to come upon the burnt-out wrecks of military vehicles and pick-up trucks. This was an area that had seen some fierce fighting, and behind the roadway on the sandy verges, lines of unmarked graves showed where the fighters from the loyalist side had been buried. Those dead amongst the rebels were treated with much more care and consideration, being buried in marked graves near their relatives if at all possible.

Some kilometres further on they came to the outer limits of the city. Here, under a concrete archway with some buildings beside it, a checkpoint had been set up. Gilbraith slowed the truck and pulled up beside the half-dozen inquisitive looking rebel soldiers that manned it.

'Allah ahakbar, allikum.'

'Allah Alikum,' came back the response with the customary touch to the breast with the right hand.

'Have you seen a ten-ton Iveco lorry come through here in the last hour or so, with maybe five or more people in the cab?'

One of the rebels nodded, 'Yes we let them through. They said they were carrying vital hospital supplies.'

'Did you check out the cargo?'

'No, we looked in the back. Just a lot of yellow drums with "Hospital Supplies"

stencilled on them. Their paperwork was in order, so we let them go.'

'Oh well, you just allowed some of the most diehard Gaddafi supporters through with some toxic shit on board which they're going to use in their rockets!'

The faces of the young rebel soldiers fell.

'They're only about a hour ahead of you. You can catch them before they get to the Al Safrah oasis.'

Gilbraith touched his breast in the classic Arabic gesture of reconciliation and climbed back into the truck. We sped off in a northerly direction, the edge of Tripoli disappearing further and further into the murk of the detritus blown up by the dust of the truck. There was no other traffic on the tarmacked road that ran like a black snake through the red and yellow sand and sand-stone bluffs, and never-ending undulating dunes that stretched out like a billowing sheet that had been left to dry in the cruel and blistering sun. In these parts in the height of summer the temperature can easily top 40 degrees, and the hot and searing wind generated by the passage of the truck did nothing to cool the passengers. The air con on the truck had long given up the ghost, and the sweat was pouring off the faces of the passengers. I hoped the walnut dye Jim had used on us would stand this test. He assured me it would last a good long time. How long I wanted to know. Did I fancy the Arab-swarthy look once I got back to Scotland? Assuming I'd get back. His reply shocked the crap out of me. The dye's permanent. It can take up to a year to finally remove itself from the epidermal layer. So, a good washing with pears gentle soap is about as much good as trying to scrape it off with a pan scourer. Catriona looked a bit shocked as well, but her natural beauty can take it whereas, I didn't want the epithet of "wee toolie bum kich" shouted after me as I strolled back through my Gorbals neighbourhood. Well, I was stuck with it. These thoughts had somewhat taken the edge off my fear, and as the sun started to sink lower into the desert we came upon the desert oasis of al Safrah. This was your typical desert watering hole. A group of single-storey mud dwellings dominated by a slightly larger mosque, all grouped around an enticing-looking date palmed area, where women were collecting water and a few goats and camels were being watered by their herdsmen. A group of camouflaged-dressed rebel soldiers with Kalashnikovs slung nonchalantly over their shoulders strolled about. Of the ten-ton Iveco truck there was no sign. Jim asked after them to be told that they had passed through an hour ahead of us. Having first fuelled up with diesel and water, we decided there was little point in chasing them through the night. They'd most likely pull off the road to sleep anywhere and then we'd miss them. The chase was on for the morning. There was still a good three-hundred miles to go till we hit Sabha. We asked a village elder where we could stay and were directed to the oasis guesthouse. In true Arab hospitality style the elders invited us to a meal, and the women of the village started to prepare a goat stew and couscous tagine cooked on a thorn branch wood fire in front of the village mosque. As the sun sank into the pink of the desert sand, the villagers gathered around the fire. The multiple tagines were opened, and the tantalising smell of goat stew mingled with the acrid smell of the fire. We helped ourselves in the time-honoured fashion by hand,

and never has a meal seemed so civilised and delicious. The conversation swung back and forth first, the war, and how it had impinged on this desolate outpost of desert life. The villagers had seen con trails in the sky as NATO planes swept over to bomb Shaba, but as for ground forces they had seen none until the rebel soldiers had appeared in a couple of pick-up trucks with 35mm anti-aircraft guns mounted in the truck beds. The latest news from Tripoli and the towns along the coast was poured over with great interest, but the war had hardly been noticed here. I asked if Gadaffi's men holed up in Shaba had passed through. There was a general collective head shaking and the consensus was that no new troops other than the existing garrison had passed by on their way to Shaba. No news of the Brother Leader either. His tricksey slide away and hide attitude, where he was never known to be in one place for longer than 24 hours, had not endeared him to any of the villagers, even though they came from the same Bedouin roots as Gadaffi. Someone said he'd spend the nights sleeping in hospitals to avoid the NATO bombing. Others that he had holed up in the Great Man-Made River, which had a tarmacked road bed capable of taking wheeled vehicles for a great part of its length. This seemed to be the preferred escape route and there was much sucking of teeth and shaking of heads as the village men discussed the facts, and they generally reckoned he was over the border in Niger and would conduct a never-ending terrorist and guerrilla war from there until he was eventually killed or captured.

I felt my eyelids start to droop and the ashy fire in front of me became two and I knew it was time for bed. Catriona and I wished the others good night and made our way to the guesthouse. The bed was an acacia wood frame with willow strakes to hold up the goat wool woven palliasse, stuffed with wool, and quite the most comfortable and sumptuous bed we had lain in for some time. Out like a light the both of us, and awoke many hours later completely refreshed to a bright desert morning and the Imman calling the faithful to prayer.

We breakfasted on the most delicious bowls of goat's milk yogurt, flavoured with wild bees honey and ultra fresh flat bread just out of the village ovens. By 9 a.m. we were fully ready to take up the chase again, and having filled the truck with fuel and water we headed back onto the black top and into the unknown.

The terrain started to take on a sinister, more open aspect, as we drove through the area marked on the map as the Sea of Sand: marching dunes topped with shallow outcrops of dark stones. This landscape stretched endlessly into the distance on either side of the road. Ahead, on a slight rise, a burnt-out ten ton truck lay on its axles. It wasn't from this war, but from the conflict that had raged through here sixty years ago when Hitler had wanted to rule the world. I gazed with astonishment at it and its old-fashioned looking styling. It looked as if it had been hit yesterday, not sixty years ago. Then we were past and barrelling into the distance. The air temperature was rising again, and before long the sweat was pouring off us. Suddenly the truck gave an almighty lurch to the left, crashed off the tarmac and skidded to a stop on its side. We were thrown about in the cab, the interior mirror slashed my face from forehead to mouth corner, and warm blood trickled down it. Catriona gave a groan and her walnut skinned face turned pale. Jim just about managed to hold onto the wheel. Of the other two in the flat bed there was no sign. We climbed out. The back offside tyre was completely shredded and the stub axle looked badly damaged.

'Holy shit and Christ,' Galbraith said as he took in the damage. 'Where are Khali and Aiden?'

We looked back up the road. Coming towards us, and none-the-worse for wear, the figure of a dust-covered Aiden Bathhurst. Of Corp. Smith there was no sign, but then I saw a huddled figure lying on the sand verge. He was ominously still. I ran over. He gave a groan, not dead then thank Christ. His arms and legs were cut and bruised from his ejection out of the truck, and he had struck his head on the tarmac as he rolled clear. Otherwise his injuries were less than he could have expected. Catriona was nursing her left arm and a nasty blue bruise and swelling was coming up around her wrist. She could move her arm so we reckoned it wasn't broken, and Jim soon had it strapped up and in a sling. He dealt with me in the time-honoured way with a good washing in antiseptic and some very natty field dressings that pulled the wound together like stitches. We stood in a line, the walking wounded, and contemplated the truck.

'Stub axle looks fucked.' We gazed on it. 'No wait a mo: its only a bit of crap got stuck on it. I think it should be OK. Lets pull this fucker back on its feet and we'll wap on the spare and we're off.'

Jim quickly organised some rope, and fixing it to the side of the flat bed we pulled in unison, and with a great creaking and smell of over-heated oil the truck fell back with a clang onto its three good tyres. We manhandled the hydraulic jack out of the metal box on the back, and jacked her up. The spare we fixed in minutes, and after checking to see that the machine gun was still intact by the simple expedient of firing a few rounds out of it, we were back on the road again. Not much chat now as we each contemplated how close we'd come to a much more serious accident. For the next five miles Jim drove in a sedate manner, never getting the truck much over fifty. The stub axle seemed to be functioning as it should and after about fifty more miles of monotonous black top travel, we saw ahead of us a brick building nestling on the side of the road under the shade of some acacia trees. Three rebel soldiers in the ubiquitous sand camo trousers and red and yellow tees sat at a metal table in the shade. There were enamel signs advertising Fanta, diesel and food. We pulled to a halt and disembarked. The usual greetings: Allah Akbar, Allah alikum, were exchanged with the courtesy of the right hand touching the breast. We went into the café. A large ceiling fan barely disturbed the air. A Swarthy fat man with a grey djellaba covered in a linen apron stood behind a Formica counter working his way through a pile of mint tea glasses. We ordered tea, and sat to discuss our next moves. As soon as he heard our English voices he threw his hand in the air and shouting NATO,NATO. He rushed outside to his other customers. They crowded round and there was much smiling and backslapping and thanking for the intervention NATO had given the rebel army. We asked about the state of the war from their perspective and it turned out that they were waiting for the rest of the rebels to appear once Beni Walid had fallen. Then it was on to Shaba where a difficult battle was expected. Was there any chance we could infiltrate Shaba to do mischief before the main rebel army appeared? The chief of the rebels grinned and assured us yes it was possible, since NATO had bombed the place there were many parts of the perimeter wall that had been breeched and he didn't think they were guarded. And he'd like to come too and help along with his mates. They'd been sitting here for three days now and wanted action. We talked at length about destroying the rockets and killing the main protagonists. At this stage I began to think this was looking like some Gung ho Rambo film extravaganza. Eight soldiers, some of whom were ostensibly civilians against a thousand well armed Gaddafi loyalists trapped in a last-ditch attempt to sell their lives for the Brother Leader. I think not! However, we were charged with destroying the toxic waste and spores and if by subtle means we could do that, so much the better. We welcomed their help, and having reprovisioned both vehicles with fuel, food and water we set off in the direction of Shaba. The forlorn looking proprietor standing waving by the door to his establishment. We had nicked his only customers and God or Allah knew when another would be along. Mind you, if the whole rebel army rocked up, his days of yogurt and mint tea would have come.

We had gone about seventy miles towards Shaba and we were threading our way through some very inhospitable country. Reddish-yellow sandstone escarpments on either side of the tarmac as the road climbed into the distance. The black top wound sinuously into the hills; the desert wind blowing sand and debris across it. Suddenly from ahead came the whup, whup, whup of heavy armaments and the stone shale of the roadside erupted in a shower of debris. Jim braked to a halt and moved the pick-up out of harm's way. Mohammed in the other truck had done the same. Again came the crump of 35mm anti-aircraft fire as we were targeted. Jumping down and gathering in the shade of the hillside we considered what to do.

'This is a one off,' said Jim. 'I only count one piece of ordinance, but where is it and can we attack it?'

I offered to climb up on to the hilltop and check it out. So, feeling brave as fuck, I set off with a Kalashnikov and a pair of binos. The corporal came with me. Five minutes tough scrambling brought us to the ridge. I peered over. Not a fucking thing. Then from a hidden declivity in the rocks about a hundred yards off and well hidden by the country side, I saw the muzzle flash of the heavy weapon that had menaced us. It was obvious that they had a good visual command of the road. But they were well dug in and the chances of surprising them from the road was minimal, though a rear assault on foot could be a different matter. Scrambling back down to the others I reported what we'd seen. Our plan then evolved, and it meant most of us stalking around the desert to get behind their gun emplacement. Once there, a straightforward attack with RPGs and grenades should finish them off; surprise being all. Again, the multiple crump of 35 mm ordinance filled the air and more rock and shale was sprayed across the road.

We tooled up and set off across the terrain towards our enemy, whom we assumed were Gaddafi loyalists and a forward outpost from Shaba. This time it took us much longer to get behind them, but after climbing right up onto the ridge we were able to peer down onto their positions. A small, open-ended quarry commanding the road ahead and used by the road builders, was being used now by the artillery that had fired on us.

A pick-up truck, Hyundai this time, but with a fearsome looking 35 mmm AA gun on the flat bed was backed up with its barrel pointing back down the road. A team of smart-looking Gaddafi soldiers dressed in sand camo uniforms were feeding shells into the magazine, whilst an officer strutted around shouting orders. Nothing odd in this, but when I focussed the binos on to the soldiers it became obvious that these were all women. I relayed that info to Catriona who shrugged and informed me that these bastards were deadlier than the male, and anyway she was going to kill them. Jim raised his arm, and pulling down in the classic gesture our attack began.

Three RPGs straight at the truck, and a fusillade of rifle fire from the rebels, and the SAS decimated the glamour girls before us. Suddenly there were only three soldiers left standing and they were crying out that they surrendered. We scrambled down the slope and took control of the gun and pick-up truck. The women soldiers looking shocked and tear-stained were shackled with cable ties and left in the shade. We checked out the pick-up, and minimal damage had been done in our attack, so we backed it out of its gun pit and added it to our armoury. I got behind the wheel. Catriona beside me in the cab and trooper Bathhurst on the gun in the back. Now there were three and feeling like Monty on the drive to El Alamien, we let in the clutches and shot off up the road. That 35mm gun nestling in the hillside and crewed by some of the female battalion of Gaddafi loyalist women had quite shaken me, and the others, I felt. They kept talking about it as if it were somehow more significant. After all, we had all been under the impression that the female battalions were just an example of Gaddafi's overweening arrogance and pride in being able to command beautiful female soldiers, and were purely for show. We never expected them to fight! But then backs to the wall and all that! In the distance we were able to discern the smoky overlay of a large city as the cooking fire smoke discoloured the air. Our convoy drew off the road. Catriona fired up her laptop and brought up the google earth map of Shaba. It was an extensive city with two airfields and a network of roads running in and out of the place. Approximately two-hundred-thousand souls lived here: many soldiers and airmen, and the surrounding countryside was under cultivation by agriculturalists aided by unending water from the Great Man-Made River Scheme. So a substantial city to defend, and one we knew not how many of the inhabitants were loyal to the Brother Leader, or would they prove as eager to fade away as their brothers in Tripoli when the guns came rolling by?

Jim took a look at the google page and said, 'This is bound to be road blocked. We need the Fezzan Base, and that's out to the south see here.' He pointed a meaty finger to the south of the page where a substantial heavily-walled enclosure ringed a large area of desert. Within the walls could be seen various single-storey buildings, an airstrip and other installations. Roadways snaked up to the sandstone bluffs that edged one side of the site and stopped dead. 'Those must be the Grad rocket stores. I bet that's where they've stashed the anthrax spores and the toxic waste. We need to get in there and destroy that whole area.'

I looked sceptical. 'What with: the tactical nuclear weapon I've got stashed in my underpants?'

'No way Davie lad. You keep that for Catriona!' He guffawed.

She blushed and said, 'What is your plan then Sergeant Jim?'

He suddenly looked serious. 'Well, I thought we could get into the site. Steal a Grad rocket truck and fire if off into the parking cave. That'd have the right effect, and in the confusion we might be able to destroy some ICBMs and some gantries. What do you think?'

Madness? But then the simplest plans are often the best, and this was a simple plan. We also agreed that if we could acquire Gaddafi loyalist uniforms we stood more chance of getting away with the plan, and more important getting away with our lives in the aftermath of any huge explosion the like of the ones we hoped to create. Mohammed and his two friends listened attentively to Jim as he outlined the plan and acknowledged it with huge grins and high fives. They were on side at any rate.

Chapter Thirteen

We determined to wait until nightfall as there was less chance of discovery in the dark. This was a dangerous time; there were few anti-Gaddafi forces anywhere near Sabha and we stood out like a sore thumb, our little convoy. We found a quiet back street with high walls on either side, and no buildings overlooking us and we hunkered down there for the rest of the day. Jim and Khalil wandered off into the souk and returned with flat bread, tahini sauce and falafels for us all which we avidly scoffed.

Night fell and it was time to move. We had hardly gone a hundred metres up the main road when ahead, illuminated under strong floodlights, there was a roadblock. Manned by loyalist soldiers in smart regular army uniforms and overseen by a strutting poppycock of an officer with a peaked hat and a lot of sparkly stuff on his epaulettes. He raised his arm in the time-honoured stop gesture and Jim shot him through the head with his silenced Koch pistol. The other soldiers got the same treatment from the other two SAS men. The roadblock was suddenly unmanned, and we had our uniforms. We transformed ourselves from rebel fighters in to Gaddafi loyalists, and although some of the uniforms were blood-spattered, they didn't show up under the streetlights. We dragged the bodies into the dark and piled rubbish and crap on them to hide them from prying eyes and pye-dogs. We set off again. This time our confidence soared. Suddenly we had every right to be cruising the night-time streets of Shaba, and we made our way out towards the barracks and the bluffs where the scientists were working their fiendish magic. The road skirted round the perimeter of the base and climbed up towards the sandstone bluffs. The wall was a reinforced concrete structure at least three metres high and in places it had been breeched by NATO bombing. There were no guards. We stopped high up by one such breech and peered in. Laid out before us, and seemingly oblivious to our spying, the whole of the industrious ants nest of the Gaddafi loyalist gantry-building section of the army at work. Several hundred men and women toiling over the erection of ICBM rocket gantries. They had already finished three and they were frantically working on another. A huge articulated Zill truck with a low loader back, on which lay a forty-foot long Duodong rocket. Its warhead removed. I realised with a chill in my heart that this could be the vehicle to deliver the deadly anthrax spores over an unsuspecting European city. I looked about for a facility where the soldiers might be arming the warhead. There ahead and nestled into the rock face was a glint of glass. I focussed my binos on it. In to clear view came the face of Al Arabi. He was gesturing to a white-coated scientist behind him, who was shaking his head. I grabbed Catriona by the arm and mouthed the name Al Arabi at her. She nodded grimly. I pulled Jim towards me and we had a crisis war meeting there and then. General consensus seemed to be to get into that building and wreak as much havoc as possible and kill Al Arabi and his scientist mates. They were the instigators of this horror weapon, and without them it was possible the rockets would never fly. Our discussion had brought us no answers, for the odds against us were truly horrendous. The rocket launching area was awash with troops all heavily armed, and the caves where the toxic waste and the grads were stored were virtually inaccessible. Then suddenly a lucky stroke of fortune favoured us, and by Christ we needed it. Out of a blue sky a NATO attack airplane screamed past. The Gaddafi soldiers started firing at it with everything they had, but their aim was sadly off as the state of the art jet, decalled in Italian air force colours, screamed into the distance leaving a trail of spent tracer falling behind it. Minutes later it reappeared, this time at a slightly lower altitude, and two black eggs dropped from pods under its wings. Again the g-force inherent in the machine kicked in, and it vanished into the haze above the city. The two bombs fell with unerring accuracy onto the two erected rocket launch gantries, blowing them and the equipment around into smithereens. Once the dust had settled and we could see what damage had ensued, it became obvious that no rockets would ever launch from those gantries. Only about two to three metres of twisted metal pyloning still stood upright. Two craters stood where once there had been living flesh. It was impossible to tell were bodies ended and debris began. At least it would have been quick! The Zill launch vehicle was upended, its tractor unit upside down, with its cab completely destroyed. The low loader with the rocket on was nowhere to be seen. It was as if it had been pulverised in the attack. A wailing of wounded, both male and female, came from the area next to the immediate impact. An ambulance was struggling up towards the scene but there was not much they could do. The sheer horror and extreme violence of the bombing run had dismayed us all. Even though these were our enemies dead on the ground ahead of us, it was still a shock.

'Now's the time to get in the caves and see what's happened to that yellow waste,' Catriona called over to me, and I concurred.

Gathering the others we scrambled over the wall and down towards the devastation of the launch area. Soldiers of both sexes were milling about in an aimless way, still stunned from the ferocity of the attack. It was a moment's work to commandeer a jeep. We climbed aboard and Jim gunned the engine and headed up the steep incline towards the mouth of the caves. No one tried to stop us, and we pulled up safely in the lee of what looked like a reinforced concrete door that would seal off the caves in the event of an attack. There were no personnel anywhere in the first cave. In fact it was empty of anything at all, but back against the rear wall there was another huge double door.We drove down, stopped, and cocking our weapons moved towards these doors. There was a small entry door set into the main double doors and this creaked open as we tried the handle. Still no one challenged us. Then we were in. A brightly lit aircraft-hanger-sized area completely full of Grad rocket launcher lorries, and stacked against an end wall hundreds and hundreds of the deadly inaccurate rockets the Great Brother Leader was so fond of sending against his civilian population. I could see a bright yellow-coloured drum that had been rolled away from the wall, where the rest of the Gruinard consignment was stored. Staring at this I was immediately overcome with a feeling of déjà vu, and also a feeling that at last our mission was coming to an end. How wrong I was!

We got into a defensive huddle to discuss this, like a rugby team at half time. Jim reckoned a series of plastic charges at suitable spots around the cave would bring it all tumbling down. I went for a more gung ho approach, obliterating the place with a grad rocket launch from one of the many launchers that was parked there. Catriona thought that a rocket attack might spread the toxic waste far and wide, and upon reflection I agreed. So it was with some trepidation that we left it in the hands of the professionals. Jim and Khali set to work. From their backpacks they removed slabs of grey inert plastic explosive and handfuls of detonators. Moving swiftly around the cave walls at every hundred metres or so they would insert a slab into the rock face or up against a vehicle and move on to the next location. In half an hour they had covered the whole cave. The plastic detonators were activated by an electronic message from a mobile phone or satnav device.

Jim called us all together and said, 'This is going to be one hell of a fucking explosion. We better get out of here and well away before I detonate it. We need to be up behind the wall again. There's a bit of shelter there. There's more ordinance here than I've ever seen and its going to blow Shaba to hell and back.'

Lovely, I thought: I like a good explosion, especially a vicarious one like a tower block coming down on the telly, so I was anticipating this with some excitement.

We moved back to the entrance of the second cave. I stuck my head round the inner door. A blaze of bullets shattered the quiet, and a stitching of holes appeared in the doorframe. Shit, whilst we been complacently talking and putting the plastic into place Al Arabi and his men had stealthily crept up on us and now had us pinned down. More automatic fire in the direction of the doorway, then silence.

A disembodied voice through a megaphone echoed through the first cave.

'Surrender now and no harm will come to you!'

Fat chance, with this ruthless crew. Surrender was tantamount to pulling out your own toenails when all you wanted was a soft manicure. I shuddered and stuck the barrel of my gun through the door. I gave it a three-second spray. When the noise and dust had settled, all I could hear was a hollow laugh echoing through the cave.

'No good Davie! I'm afraid your time is up. You've got thirty seconds to throw down your weapons and come out with your hands up!'

The megaphone clicked off leaving silence.

Jim tugged on my shirt, 'Listen mate, they've got us cold. But if we detonate this explosive it'll put the shit amongst the pigeons and in the confusion we might get away; all who survive that is! Gather round. On the count of three I'll detonate. There'll be a one-second gap before the electronics hit in then there'll be an almighty flash and bang. Don't hang about. It's everyone for themselves. Get through that door and spread out. The shock wave may knock us down. Fire as you run. Maximum confusion is the order of the day. Every one OK with this?'

We nodded. I clasped hold of Catriona's hand and gave it a squeeze. She squeezed back. The look in her eyes was not one I hope to see again in a long time.

The megaphone voice boomed back into the cave. 'Time's up Davie. Come out now!'

'Chew on this you bastards!' shouted Jim Gilbraith, as he activated the electronic detonators on the plastic explosive stashed around the cave walls.

For a moment there was silence, then the most horrendous explosion, rolling and spewing dirt and stones and then the stored grads started to ignite, the noise and smoke increased exponentially and the hot wave of high explosive and cave debris shot me off my feet and blew the entrance doors down. I scrambled up, and slamming the safety onto to automatic, charged like a weedy Rambo out of the first cave and into the light of the second. I was aware of my companions running alongside me, whilst Ahmed and Khali were screaming some Arabic insults as they fired from the hip towards Al Arabi's men, who were crouched down behind a pick-up truck slewed sideways on to the entrance of the cave. The whump, whump, of heavy anti-aircraft rounds coming from the pick-up suddenly stopped as Jim's accurate fire took out the gunner sitting on the gun's seat. The rolling explosion behind us kept coming. Rocks and debris stones the size of a small truck fell from the roof. The rocket launchers were exploding into flames and I realised that they were fuelled up for immediate use. We charged on. Our ploy of the ultimate confusion seemed to be working. Suddenly Al Arabi's truck revved up, and with squealing tyres shot off in a tight circle away through the doors and out into the night. We regrouped and counted casualities. Two of the rebel soldiers were gone. Khali had a bullet through his shoulder, but the rest of us had escaped with no injuries. The dust on our faces and in our hair bearing testimony as to the bad place we'd been. Behind us there was a significant rumble and the whole of the cave structure suddenly collapsed burying grads and toxic waste and, I hoped, the anthrax spores.

'Let's get out of here before the fucking lot comes down,' I screamed, as we came out into the artificial light of the floods and searchlights below. Hundreds of soldiers were looking up at the cave complex and at the clouds of dust and debris that was roiling out of the mouth of the cave like some bad-tempered dragon giving vent to its anger. They hadn't realised then that we were the cause of the explosion and just thought it must be either an accident or even a NATO strike. No sounds of Kalashnikovs firing up at us. We crept away like naughty children back towards the concrete wall that surrounded the place. The darkness descended once we got out of the glare of the launch lights. Catriona's satnav phone bleeped. She answered it, and after a few grunts and OK, she replaced the receiver.

'NATO air strike in five minutes. They're gonna take out the whole of the launch area. The rebels are advancing on Shaba and the battle for this town is about to begin.' She brushed her hand across her mouth wiping dust and grime away. I grinned a look of love at her. I got one back, and felt content.

Chapter Fourteen

We hadn't got behind the concrete wall surrounding the compound by seconds when a screaming banshee shriek of jet fighters shot overhead. There were three of them, and they came back like the avenging horsemen of the apocalypse. The first run was a recce, the second and third bombed and strafed the compound. Huge craters, where once had stood concrete buildings, appeared as if by magic as the full power of the NATO war machine was brought to bear. The Gaddafi troops within the compound shot back at the aircraft with all they had: twin-barrelled 35mm anti-aircraft guns bellowing and rocking on the back of pick-up trucks, tracer rounds lazily spiralling into the air; ineffective against the sheer speed of their opponents. Then they were gone, leaving the dust to settle and the cries of the wounded to ring hollowly across the compound. I lifted my head from my arms and peered out at the scene below. It was obvious they were done for. A few soldiers milled about in a shell-shocked way, picking through the remnants of their weaponry and equipment. The compound was a littered mess with pieces of rubble, screwed up lumps of metal, pools of blood and bits of body lying in the slowly-settling dust. Then from far off in the town itself we could hear the crackle of small arms fire as the rebels started their longed-for assault. It hadn't taken them long to get up to Shaba, but if it hadn't been for the NATO strike and our own small input it would have taken them much longer. The end game had started. Or so I thought!

'Hands up!' A scatter of automatic rifle fire at our feet. Suddenly we were surrounded by Gaddafi soldiers. They had crept up on us as we watched the devastation of the bombing raid. Their leader was none other than Mohamed Al Arabi himself, grinning his shark's grin, his diamond teeth sparkling in the artificial light. He shouted in triumph at us. 'Now you are our hostages out of here. We'll take you across the border into Niger when we go. You will act as our safe passage! The rebels will let us pass.' He laughed his horrible laugh bringing back the memory of my time in his hands in the warehouse in Glasgow so long ago. Then to compound the horror, he took out his silver-plated colt 45 pistol, walked up to our SAS companions and cold bloodedly shot the three of them in the head.

'Too many to look after. It is written. Allah is great!' He holstered his gun, giving orders to his men to bind us. They clipped our hands with cable ties and shuffled us towards the back of a pick-up truck.

I threw up. Catriona looked as pale as she had before the application of the walnut dye and it seemed as if the game was over for us.

They drove us to a part of the compound we had not seen before where a dozen four- by-four Range Rovers, top of the market stuff, were drawn up ready to leave. We were hustled into the back of one of them, with a strong-looking, oily-smelling muscular Arab with a semi automatic rifle pointed at us. We had no option but to obey. The convoy set off. Al Arabi was in the front of our vehicle and he turned his shark's mouth smile on us.

'You Davie, and you Catriona, have caused us endless trouble, right from the outset of this project. But now I have you, and you'll not escape. You are the safe passage to Niger, where we join the Brother Leader and then on to Chad or Burkino Faso. The war is not finished yet. These cars are full of wealth!' he boasted.

The convoy of white Range Rovers scuttled through the dark, away from the devastation that had become Shaba.

I asked him what he meant, and his reply was most illuminating. For months now all over Libya Gaddafi had stashed get away vehicles. He knew his time was up and he made provision. His wife and daughter and three of his sons had already escaped into Tunisia, and many of Gaddafi's top generals and advisors had already fled to neighbouring countries that would offer them asylum. In order to facilitate this, convoys of vehicles, like the one we were in, had been loaded with currency, gold bars and other negotiable wealth that would ease their passage south or north. At one stage Gaddafi had offered £126,000 to each farmer who would swear allegiance to him and leave his house available for the Brother Leader to use. Consequently, right across the tribal desert heartland were safe houses where Gaddafi and his top advisors knew they would be safe. To them it was only a question of making it safely from one to another before crossing a border into another country and disappearing. Never mind the rhetoric about dying on the sacred soil of the country he loved. Pragmatic as ever, he'd made his plans. The fact that Al Arabi was utilising these was a bonus for him. But in the chaos of the final stages of the war, who knew what was happening.

Our convoy sped through the night, the moonlight reflecting off the white painted vehicles. No NATO planes saw us, and by late into the night we had pulled up in a remote desert oasis farm. This was one of Gaddafi's safe houses, and the farmer came out to greet us. After the usual Allah Akbahs and deep salaams, he obsequiously led us forward into the building he called home. Several women and children were gathered there, and a steaming pot of rice and lamb stew was placed on a low table. Al Arabi's crew set to with a will cramming their faces with the food. Catriona and I looked on from our corner of the room, saliva dribbling from our mouths as the tantalising smells of the food tortured us. We were still cable-tied and it didn't look as if anyone was going to give us anything to eat. Then one of the women threw down a stale loaf of flat bread and placed a pitcher of water before us. Thanks darling, I thought as I tried to drink from the jug and tear a bit of bread from yesterday's loaf.

Al Arabi shot us a glance and smiled his sharks smile.

'So now you see how you like it?' This sentiment made no sense to me. I didn't like it one bit, and what's more I was determined to get my own back at the earliest opportunity.

The guards hustled us out of the farmhouse and into a small tin shed. This had been a camel stable by the smell of it. There was a small amount of acacia thorn branches on the floor and plenty of camel shit, but that was all. The guard slammed the door and I heard a padlock clunk into place on the door clasp. Now this was a predicament. How to escape from this? Our hands were tied, and we had no bedding, but we were exhausted, so huddling together for warmth on the shit-scattered floor we fell asleep.

I awoke with an excruciating pain in my back and my wrists, suddenly realising the predicament we were in. I lent down towards Catriona. She was fast asleep, but her hands were very swollen. The pinkish dawn was breaking through the velvet night and quickly the outlines of the shed we were in became more visible. It was made entirely of corrugated tin and I knew it would be an oven very shortly. So much so, that we could die in it if we weren't let out. Already the temperature was high up in the seventies and dawn had only just broken.

I shouted out. 'Water, for the love of Allah. Water!'

Catriona came awake with a groan and tried to massage her swollen hands. She was unable to as the guard had tied the cable ties so tight they had scored into her wrists.

I shouted again, 'Help!'

This time there came the sound of a gun barrel being run down the outside of the tin wall of the shed. Then blessed relief, the sound of someone opening the padlock. An Arab stood grinning in the entrance. His semi-automatic rifle pointed at us.

'Out! out!' he gestured with the gun.

We stumbled forward into the bright dawn. Al Arabi sat in the shade in a wicker chair. He took a look at us and shook his head.

'We are not savages; release them from their bonds.'

One of the Arabs stepped forward and cut through the cable ties binding us. As the blood flowed back into our wrists and hands the pain was excruciating and Catriona cried out in agony. I reached forwards to comfort her and got a thwack around the head with the barrel of a gun. I fell to the floor, blood streaming from my scalp.

'Give them water,' Al Arabi commanded his men.

A scummy-looking jug of tepid water was thrust at me. I drained it. Never had champagne tasted as good and the curative effects were instant. I felt some strength and hope flow through my body. Another jug was brought for Catriona, and I could see the same thing happening to her.

Al Arabi said, 'Today, we are making our way into the mountains. We will take the Salvador pass towards Afon Adra Bous and over the border into the Air mountains And then no one shall find us.' He gave a maniacal cackle, and for the first time I realised the man was mad. He gave orders to shackle us up again and once that was done we were bundled into the back of one of the Range Rovers, and the convoy set off towards the Niger Libyan border. From my knowledge of the geography and the look of the terrain I thought we were likely 600 to 700 km from the border, so a good day's travel ahead. Time to mull over an escape plan! I tried to talk to Catriona but the guard made the universal gesture for silence and menaced me with his gun. I shut up.

The ground ahead was exactly the same as the ground behind. Low shale-like deposits on the top of wind-blown sand dunes stretching in every direction. Not another human in sight; not another animal or vehicle. We could have been on the moon apart from the heat, which was beginning to build into an unpleasant high 40 degrees. This was indeed the dead heart of the Libyan desert, and all in the convoy were only too eager to get through it. On the side of the tarmac, faint tracks made by nomadic Arabs and their flocks meandered back and forth in a confusing directionless manner, and I realised that without local knowledge or a guide, any traveller would be hopelessly lost in moments and fried to death in the oven-hot temperatures. The air con in the cars was doing its best to keep pace with the mounting outdoor temperature, but the guard was feeling it. Sweat was pouring from his face, and a very unpleasant smell of body odour and human excrement was coming off him.

He didn't seem to notice, but I did all right. Catriona had closed her eyes, and I followed suit, and very soon I had fallen into a shallow sleep.

I awoke some hours later. The heat was as intense, but now the terrain had changed remarkably. The horrid shaley dunes had given way to a sandstone escarpment that ran as far as the eye could see from east to west along the horizon. At one point a startlingly green area of vegetation stood out from the uniform pinky- grey of the sandstone. Palm trees, and a few white buildings could be seen nestling against the wall of the rock face. Our convoy made its way towards this oasis, and pulled up in front of a palm-lined well area where a few nomadic camel herders were watering their animals. Once the dust had settled and the burnouses were pulled back from the heat, the usual greetings were given with hand shakes all round. Not for us though. Al Arabi and his men were settling to an evening meal of couscous and camel meat stew. We had not eaten for at least twenty-four hours and my stomach was as hollow as a politician's rhetoric.

I called out to Al Arabi, 'Any chance of food; you'll starve us to death otherwise?'

He laughed, 'Save me some bullets!' He gave orders and his men brought us a bowl of stew and some flat bread. It was gone in seconds and the bowls licked clean.

We were shackled up again, and hustled into a mud hut building. This one had two beds in it and looked like a basic guesthouse accommodation for visitors. It was a definite improvement on last night's bed and breakfast. What's more, the guard locked us in and stood away from the building, giving us our first chance to talk and work out what to do.

Catriona said, 'This is a dangerous pickle we're in Davie me boy. Al Arabi's going to kill us for sure. We've got to get away. Any ideas?'

I shook my head, and then it came to me in a blinding flash. I outlined the plan to her and although there was an initial reluctance, she soon realised that this was perhaps our only chance.

'OK then. In the morning we do it.'

We kissed and selecting a bed apiece lay down on them with some excitement coursing through our bodies.

I didn't sleep well, tossing and turning though the night as I thought over how our plan might go wrong. Shortly before dawn, I fell asleep, and by the time the guard had unlocked us I was extremely bleary eyed. In an unreal daze, I moved forward to the doorway.

'Here John, I need a shit.' I mimed the act of defecating and his eyes lit up with understanding.

Catriona called out as well, 'I do too.'

The guard gestured us out of the building and pointing his rifle escorted us out of the oasis towards an area of dunes behind the buildings. It was still very quiet. The rest of the villagers had not yet risen, but as the sun heated up it was only a few minutes away from the start of the day and moments left to fulfil our plan.

I saw Catriona start to unbutton her djellaba top, and she shrugged it off exposing her breasts to the morning sun. The guard clocked it, and his eyes glazed over. Reaching out like a child in a sweet shop, he tried to fondle her breasts. I jumped him and slipped my cabled hands over his neck. With a strength born out of desperation, I started to throttle him. It was surprisingly easy and as the sweat poured down my face and neck he gave a shudder and blood spurted from his ruptured trachea. He slumped to the ground and his arterial blood flowed into the sand.

Hardly a sound had passed our lips. The guard shuddered once and gave up the ghost. I eased him down on to the sand and picked up his Kalishnikov.

'You're a better shot with this than I ever am; let's get into some cover and see what damage we can do to these bastards.'

Catriona nodded. We cut our cable-tied hands, and frisking the dead body for weapons and ammo we collected about fifty rounds in a bandolier from around the guard's shoulder and a very nice pearl-handled colt revolver, which I stuffed into my waistband. We crept away towards the deep shadow of the escarpment. The villagers were starting to make their breakfast. They had gathered in front of the well, and having made their morning prayers to Allah, they had built a fire of acacia thorn and were frying up eggs and bread. The smells were tantalising. So much so it brought out Al Arabi and his top henchmen who hung about scratching fleas under their djellabas.

The Kalashnikov gave a flat crack and then another. Al Arabi spun away from the fire and fell sideways into it. His henchman was drilled through the head by a bullet from Annie Oakley. The other half-dozen soldiers running hither and yon, completely disorientated by the unexpected attack. Catriona clicked onto automatic and sprayed a bunch of milling uniforms. They all went down. The rest of the villagers scattered into the undergrowth and we had the oasis to ourselves.

Slowly walking forward towards the carnage we checked out the dead and wounded. There were three slightly wounded soldiers with superficial flesh wounds, which would have debilitated action on their part. And the boss, Al Arabi – dead. His shark like teeth no longer gleaming like some <u>Sarowoski</u> crystal show. This man, who had haunted us, who had tortured me, and insulted Catriona, who had cold-bloodedly shot the three SAS soldiers. Dead! The wounded soldiers we forced into the first Range Rover, and we told the only one with a smattering of English and some pigeon French to drive away and never come back on pain of death. We stripped the car and their persons of any useful weapons, and blasted off a magazine of automatic fire into the air. They got the message, and were last seen high-tailing it towards the Niger border. The inhabitants of the oasis flocked round us and with much Allah Akbar and salaams offered us eggs, bread and tea. In a mixture of French, sign language and the occasional English and Italian word, we came to realise that these were rebel supporters and only too pleased to see the back of Gaddafi's men who had been pouring through the oasis for weeks now on their rat-run to safety in Niger.

We checked out the vehicles. Of the dozen that we had set out with there were three or four, four-wheeled brand new state of the art Range Rovers with satnavs and GPS positioning gizmos, equipped with car-to-car radios. We selected the two newest and most robust looking ones, and stripping the others of their diesel and water containers, loaded them into the two cars. In the back of each car, a locked safe had been fitted. Once we broke those open it became obvious that here was a fortune stashed. In one, about thirty kilos of 22 carat red gold. In another, in small grey suede bags, fifty to a hundred in each bag and there were at least ten bags: uncut diamonds from the diamond fields of Nigeria. But it was in the last car that the real cornucopia was revealed: currency notes; hundreds and hundreds of bundles of US dollar bills in 100 dollar denominations. Bundles of fifty-pound notes, Euros and Dhirrams, and a plethora of other lesser-known currency including South African rands and Russian roubles. Here was enough money to help out the quantative easing the banks in Britain were about to undertake. We transferred the lot into our vehicles. This seemed like a legitimate perk to us. We talked about it, but very soon it was obvious that this new wealth was ours to spend! We donated the remaining cars to the villagers and with much waving, wailing and Allahing, we set off back in the direction we had come yesterday. I drove the lead car, and Catriona brought up the second. We were chattering nonstop on the car-to-car radio as we planned our next moves. We were free: free from Al Arabi, free from the terror of captivity; speeding back towards Tripoli and the Mary Swift. Our discussion had quickly led us to the conclusion that a nice Mediterranean cruise wouldn't come amiss, and that if we stashed the money and gold and diamonds in a Swiss bank account we could live high on the hog for ever. So we decided there and then to get back to the boat and head off across the Med to Monte Carlo where I was sure we'd find a branch of a very secretive Swiss bank that would handle our ill-gotten gains. Catriona suggested that there was very little point in having two cars, and I concurred. At the first suitable spot, which happened to be close to Shaba; that ill treated town where such devastation had been wreaked, we pulled off the road and transferred all the goodies, water and diesel from one car to the other. This was much better, and gave us a chance each to catch up on our sleep whilst the other one drove. So this is what we did, and as the miles of black top disappeared under our wheels I day dreamed the day dreams of the avaricious. Occasionally glancing back at my loved one, fast asleep on the rear seat of the luxury car courtesy of the Brother Leader. Traffic built up as we drew closer and closer to the capital, and normal life in Libya began to assume top priority. We were pulled over twice at roadblocks, but our British passports were sufficient to pass us through with much joyful calling of NATO, NATO and Cameron, Cameron. After a non-stop journey of twenty-four hours, we pulled into the quay side at Tripoli Harbour. Circling round towards the wharf where the Mary Swift was moored we looked out for the dear boat. Nothing. The wharf where we had left her was completely deserted. Bleary eyed and slightly worried, we tracked down the harbour master's office and confronted the official whose job it was to run this great harbour.

'Where's our boat?' was my first question.

He shrugged an oily shrug. 'What boat effendi?'

'The one that we left here ten days ago, tied up secure at the wharf.'

I described the Mary Swift to him and a big smile broke out across his face.

'Oh that boat. Impounded for non-payment of harbour dues. There is a daily charge,

and if the owner doesn't pay or can't pay, the boat is impounded until the time the dues are paid.'

'How much?' I enquired.

He brought out an electronic calculator from his desk drawer and proceeded to hit in a series of numbers.

'100 Libyan dinars a day for ten days, plus moving charges and mooring fees one- thousand, three-hundred dinars please Effendi.'

He almost held his hand out there and then. I scuttled off back to the car and pulled out a few thousand Libyan dinars from our huge stash. Counting out the exact amount I returned to the office and gave it to the harbour master. His smile split his face again and soon he was ushering us across the harbour to an area where various craft, the Mary Swift included, where tied up.

She seemed none-the-worse for wear and her engine fired up first time, and we gratefully eased her away from her Tripoli prison and moored her again next to the car. Empting the car and stashing our new wealth in the under-sole secret compartment, along with two rifles and two revolvers, took the best part of an hour. Then we drove into town and stocked up with food for our journey: fresh tomatoes, potatoes, couscous and rice. Two bottles of bushmills, several tins of evaporated milk, some fresh onions and carrots completed our stocks. Not for choice, but because that was all the supermarket stocked. The fighting was over in the capital but it was still taking time for the full panoply of life to re-establish itself. However, the place was a bustle with many people going about their legitimate business. Traffic streamed up the main harbour road, and the sounding of car horns was a blessed change from the sound of anti-aircraft fire. We made our way to a roadside café and had a reviving glass of mint tea, and then back to the boat. Every thing was well with the Mary Swift, but being so heavily laden with money, gold and diamonds, we took no chances and moored out away from the wharf in the shallow inner harbour. A very restful night was had, apart from the strenuous activity of our love making as Catriona and I celebrated our release from danger, and what we hoped would be the start of our brand new life together. Wrong again!

The bleeping of the satellite phone in its cage on the bulkhead wall brought me back into the land of the living. Sun was streaming in from the porthole in our cabin, and I reluctantly swung my legs to the floor. It hardly seemed as if a minute had passed since we fell exhausted to sleep.

I glanced at my watch: half-eight in the morning. What bastard calls at half-eight in the morning?

'That bastard called Angus, that's who, Davie my boy.' His bonhomie grated with me at that time in the morning.

'I'm not your boy,' I spat at the phone.

'My, oh my. Oh yes you are. You signed that piece of paper mind, and we own you lock, stock and barrel. Now listen up. The killer of Yvonne Fletcher?'

His voice had taken on a much more serious tone. I listened hard. He has agreed to spill the beans and admit his guilt in exchange for immunity and a million in diamonds in a Swiss bank account.

'You and my sister have been chosen as the couriers. Non-attributable MI6 operative, you know!'

I hardly needed to nod: I grunted instead.

'So what's in it for us, if we do this for you?' There was an ominous silence then. 'You get to keep the stash you pulled out of that Gaddafi car!'

What! How did he know about that, I thought. We'd been discreet beyond discretion, but then it came to me. Satellite observation. Some greasy little operative in an office at GCHQ tracking our every movement had clocked us loading or offloading the gold and notes. Oh well, the deal sounded like a fait accompli to me. So I agreed. By now Catriona was standing beside me listening on microphone. A look of horror on her beautiful face as she realised we were not free yet of the clutches of the establishment. Angus outlined the plan. Get a bag of sparklers from our Embassy in Tripoli, take them to Switzerland to the bank designated and hand them over. Simple. Except smuggling diamonds is nearly a capital offence, at least a ten-year gaol sentence. Luckily the Swiss banking authorities were so up their own arses about secrecy that we wouldn't have much difficulty once we got into the bank. The chosen bank was in Bern, so we thought: nice sea trip to North Italy, hire a car and a drive over the Alps into Switzerland, visit the lovely city of Bern, do the business, do our business, have a few days' hols and then back on the Mary Swift and home. Reason for the boat trip: 20 kilos of gold bars and over a million in paper currency. Weighs a lot, and getting that weight through customs might be iffy in the extreme, so it's a boat trip to the north Mediterranean coast and an alpine car ride.

Later that morning, having located the British Embassy in Tripoli and obtained a tiny bag of sparklers from them and the relevant details of the transaction to the Swiss bank, we fuelled up and got as many provisions as it was possible to buy from the still very sparsely stocked food shops of Tripoli. With light hearts and hardly any regrets, we shoved off from the quay. Motoring out into the Med from the harbour area, and leaving the madness of the war behind us did us both good, and with a grin tacked to my face like a sign for 24-hour happiness, I kissed my beloved. She entered the way points that would take us across the sea to Trieste; this being the closest we could get to Switzerland, calling at Malta enroute, mainly to stock up on a few comestibles and to refuel, then up the Adriatic and dock there before hiring a car and overlanding it to Bern.

We left the coast of Libya behind and headed due north into the balmy evening air that carried the smells of the land with it: the smells of lavender and wild thyme. And the not-so-pleasant odours of the big city: traffic fumes and the cloying smells of human existence. We hoped to make landfall in Malta before the night was out and pushed the large engine of the Mary Swift. I was as competent on the wheel as I was ever going to get, and leaving the autopilot on I dropped down into the galley and rustled up a quick risotto. I'd just got it out on the plates when I heard Catriona's yell from the deck.

'Shift off you silly bugger, you'll ram us!'

I rushed on deck to see one of those slim, fast, low-lying boats the police call cigarette boats, which smugglers use to bring contraband into ports all along the Mediterranean coast. Capable of outrunning nearly anything on the sea with a top speed of over forty knots. This one was barrelling towards us at about that speed, and I could see that the two blokes in the cockpit were intent on using the guns they were pointing our way. Acting like the proverbial shit off a shovel I screamed below, ripped up the cabin sole and pulled out our Kalashnikovs and a few stooks of ammo. Above I could hear the crackle of small arms fire. I hoped to hell Catriona had taken cover. By the time I got up on deck again I found the deckhouse riddled with holes from automatic fire. I passed a rifle to Catriona, and as the cigarette boat swung about in the water to come in again for another attack, we both fired our Kalashnikovs on auto. The thin plywood sides of the speedboat erupted into splinters, and she stopped dead in the water. Holed below the waterline she started to sink. One of the occupants was slumped forward over the wheel, and the other had his hands up, and was supplicating us to save him. Throwing a life buoy in his direction, we throttled back the big engine and came to a wallowing rest. Pulling the soaking shocked man on board, he lay gasping on the deck. I kicked him savagely in the ankle.

'What the fuck are you up to you tosser?' he shrugged. Catriona clicked off the safety and pointed the rifle at him. In French, then Italian she posed the same question.

No reply was imminent. I kicked him again, and at last a stream of what I took to be some Slavonic language came out of his mouth. Neither of us understood him. I pulled him to his feet, and standing there like a bedraggled water rat I almost felt sorry for the bloke. My initial reaction was that they were after our stash of gold and diamonds having somehow gained access to the knowledge of what we were carrying. I forced him at gun point into the smallest of the three cabins and locked him in. What to do with him? After a bit of a discussion it was agreed to hand him over to the authorities in Malta. I was all for setting him adrift on a life raft, but Catriona reckoned that was too draconian and smacked of old-time piracy. The fact that the bastard had tried to kill us and would have done so if he'd got on board was neither here nor there in her morality, and after my anger at the man had simmered down I agreed. I took him some water and cable-tied his wrists together, although he looked pretty shell shocked and as if escape was the last thing on his mind. We called the authorities in Malta and reported the attack, and asked for assistance from the police once we docked to get rid of our prisoner. It transpired that there was a gang of smugglers from Slovenia and the Balkan states left over from the war, who preyed on shipping in the southern Med. And the police would love to interrogate this bloke. We chugged on; nothing untoward upon the horizon or close too. Gulls swooped and shrieked at us as we got closer to Malta. When we eventually saw the clean, grey, sandstone cliffs that surround the harbour at Valetta it was with some relief, for the attack had unnerved us somewhat and our talk was all about how did they know, what did they know, and was it likely to happen again. We moored up where the pilot boat showed us, and two burly customs officials and a couple of policemen came aboard. Our papers checked out, but they didn't like the fact that we had unlicensed guns on board until we explained about Angus, MI6 and the rest, when they reluctantly issued us with temporary onward transit visas for the weapons. They took away the very bedraggled pirate, and that was the last we saw of him. Meanwhile we treated ourselves to an expensive meal in a little harbour-side restaurant, but with our stash of money it was a mere bagatelle. The wine was over 50 euro a bottle but it complemented the squid and prawn fricassee on a bed of balsamic drizzled salad. La-di-da! Followed by chocolate ice-cream Bavarian tort, whatever that was. We both leant back from the table and sighed. Back on the boat we decided on an early night, and the land of nod had grabbed us and knocked us unconscious within minutes.

It was a late start, but we'd really been in need of the rest, and by the time the clock on Valletta harbour tower chimed twelve we were slowly negotiating our way out of the crowded roads. A lot of small pleasure craft were milling around as their owners tried to get their best money's worth from their investments. One flash bastard in a gleaming plastic 38 foot Westerly came so close to scrapping down our wale, that I was able to shout across to his very nubile companion, 'Any closer and you'd have to marry me.' This got me a look of extreme disapproval from his piggy little eyes and a smile from his companion; he had to adjust his Valetta Yacht Club tie a little.

At last we were through the throng and away into the open ocean, where a full ahead from the wheelhouse set us in the direction of the Adriatic. Weather was as good as gold; a slight sou-westerly about three knots helped us on our way. Not a cloud in the sky and the blue of it all burnt down in a never-ending warm-rayed extravaganza. Lovely!

I needn't have worried: the Almighty had something in store for us anyway, and it came roiling up over the horizon from the Albanian shore. One of those devastating black squalls that come out of nowhere in the Med and sink yachts and small boats. The blue around us changed in minutes to a murky grey and black clouds interspersed with lightening flashes covered the horizon. The sea started to get up like a startled stallion disturbed by bees, and before you could say Davy Jones' Locker we were being tossed about like the proverbial cork. Catriona was shouting orders about head-to the wind as she fought the squall. The Mary Swift was built for this sort of thing and worse, and gamely answered her tiller as her head came into the wind and she started to ride out the storm. An unending series of huge waves were rolling under her and spray was crashing over the wheelhouse. The radio crackled. 'Mayday, mayday! Pleasure yacht Orpheus out of Valetta, taking on water. In danger of broaching'. Then a series of latitude points. Catriona pushed them into the machine and a printed map spewed out of its mouth with the endangered yacht marked on it. 'Not far from us, we better see if we can help.'

She spun the wheel and the sturdy little trawler crashed through the waves towards the last-known way point of the sinking Orpheus. The weather seemed to be moderating as the dark squall fled westward. The seas were still running high and the green-flecked wave tops crashed and boomed against our hull. Then ahead we saw a dismasted hull wallowing into and out of the wave troughs. By Christ I thought, it's that tosser who nearly rammed us in the entrance to Valetta Harbour. And sure enough it was. The gleaming white plastic of the hull was sadly damaged and stoved in by the waves, and as the cockpit rose up above wave height I could see his piggy little eyes staring out in shocked horror. His nubile girlfriend, tears staining her makeup stood silently beside him. We threw him a line and he fairly deftly attached it to his boat. We reeled him in.Then he had the gall to suggest we tow the hull back to Valetta. The arrogance of the pig! No way, Hose!

'You want rescuing, we'll do it, but you'll end up in Trieste which is our next port of call. Anyway, you're insured aren't you?' A look of thwarted anger crossed his face, but we had him by the short and curlies, and reluctantly he abandoned his gin palace and he and his girlfriend climbed gingerly on board. We offered them towels to dry themselves and a shot of whisky apiece to settle themselves, then the trouble started. 'You must take us back to Valetta. What cabin can we use. I need the mobile phone!' On and on it went like the whining of a petulant child. He hadn't even introduced himself and his woman friend. He started treating us like servants. Finally I snapped. 'Listen you little Turk, (he wasn't a Turk, but a Russian oligarch it turned out)

'We 've just saved you from a watery grave and the least you can do is act a little bit humble, and maybe thank us for pulling you from the briny.'

He grinned and his whole face altered, from the unpleasant piggy little-eyed bastard throwing his weight around he suddenly became all sweetness and light.

'I am truly sorry if I give offence. My name is Serge Ovanoviff, and this is my friend Helga. Of course we are grateful that you have saved us and we will do anything we can to compensate you. But when we left Valetta and the weather was so good, I had no idea we would be in danger for our lives one hour later. I have to be on land somewhere to sign a paper that gives me control of Serge

Com, a Russian gas pipe line company, and if I can't sign I loose everything.'

'Just anywhere on land?'

'Anywhere I can get to a lawyer's office.'

We pulled out the chart of the east coast of Italy.

'Brindisi is the nearest. We could be there in an hour.'

His look of gratitude far exceeded anything I'd ever seen before and he said. 'If I could use your mobile, I'll call my office in Valetta and they can fax the papers to Brindisi. You have just saved me.' He shook my hand and then Catriona's. Helga just stood there grinning. I think she was a decorative object, a bit like a beautiful vase people could admire but whose input was limited to pleasure activities. Serge punched in a few numbers and a string of Russian came from his mouth. The call went on for some time and towards the end I could see that exasperation was setting in. But then he listened for a bit and a wide smile came over his face. He disconnected and gave Catriona her phone back.

'Good! Brindisi please' and he rubbed his fat fingers together.

By now the coast of Italy was very distinct on our port side and the polluted air above Brindisi was causing a smoggy mix that kept the port hidden. Then suddenly we were through it and the Sailor's Monument, a white marble monolith towering above the harbour and town, came into view. Brindisi is a charming town and ferry port on the south Italian coast and hosts a huge American airbase, which had been instrumental in the war in Libya as a base for NATO fighter jets. We chugged into the harbour and the pilot cutter showed us a mooring. Serge and Helga vanished into the interior of the town, but not before promising to return, and wine and dine us that evening in true oligarch style. We looked forward to it. We changed into some thing easier for the temperature, which had climbed into the top twenties and went on shore to explore. We spent a wonderful day looking at old buildings and the Roman column that marked the end of the Apennine Way from Rome to Brindisi. When the noise and bustle of the Lambretta scooters and the sheer bravado of their riders got to us we retired to a piazza and settled down under the trees with a bottle of chilled chianti and in the dappled shade we watched the never-ending to and fro of Brindisi society. Shortly before nightfall the grumpy-looking figure of Serge, with a glamorous looking Helga on his arm, hove into view. He looked sour, but his manner was far from it. Bonhomie exuded from him like toothpaste from a squeezed tube, and it wasn't long before we all knew that his gas pipeline deal had netted him somewhere close to ten million dollars. Smiling a Russian smile, whatever that is, he produced two packets from his Gucci bag and passed one to Catriona and one to me. We opened them and then our mouths fell open at the opulence of the gifts. He had presented us each with a top-of-the-range Phillipe Patak wristwatch. Catriona's was a Calatrava lady's watch in white gold retailing at over £15 thousand. Mine was a Patak Aquanoaut in rose gold, which I knew for a fact retailed at £25 grand. What a gift. We were both gob- smacked. We both said we couldn't accept such gifts, but Serge only smiled and said, 'Too late my friends they're paid for and I can't take them back.' An expressive Slavic shake of the shoulders finished the argument, and we were the proud possessors of two very expensive watches. Then Serge and Helga took us to the most expensive restaurant in Brindisi: Da Vito, a charming white-painted villa in the colonial style, just off the main pedestrian drag, where the anti pasto of octopus and lettuce leaves was hardly bettered by the mozzarella and tomato salad. Then linguine in tomato sauce, finished by a dessert to die for: raw chocolate sacher torte and clotted cream.

Replete and staggering, we returned to the Mary Swift. The others went back to their five star hotel. We fell into bed and into the arms of oblivion.

Next morning was another bright and brassy Brindisi day, with a slight sea breeze blowing in off the Adriatic. A perfect day for a cruise up the coast to Trieste. We set off at about ten o'clock and by lunchtime, when the pangs of hunger were getting the better of us, we motored into a charming white-painted village clinging to the cliffs overlooking the bay. A bottle of chilled Chianti and a plate of the local seafood salad soon revived us, and amidst the dappled shade of the restaurant courtyard we felt life couldn't get much better. Back on board we plugged in the Trieste way points and settled down on deck to catch some well-earned rays. The rest of the day passed in a pleasant haze of blue skies, summer breezes and the occasional Bushmills. Lying on the teak deck on deck chairs with the desultory chit-chat that only lovers can have, we passed the day very pleasantly. The coast of Slovenia and Isrtia passed slowly by on our starboard side as we made our sedate way towards the bustling border port of Trieste. It lies on the boundary between Slovenia and Italy and is a part of Italy. A busy, pantiled port with higgledy-piggledy houses running up and down the hillsides. An overall impression of reds and browns interspersed with numerous medieval churches. The Mediterranean sea sparkled below. Here were the mega traffic flows of a border crossing, and the main point for Slovenian lorries of the soft-sided variety to cross with their goods into Italy. We had decided to stop here for our onward journey into Switzerland as a cheaper alternative to mooring in Venice, which is hugely expensive on harbour charges, whereas Trieste, though expensive is at least affordable.

We collected a pilot cutter and two policemen, who oversaw us into a berth. The policemen, both fashion-plates with immaculate, clean and knife-creased, pressed uniforms who spent their time with us looking at one another and themselves from behind their mirror shades. They were perfunctory in their searches and failed to find any of the contraband we were carrying, which would have opened us up to many years in goal. At last, having exhausted all opportunities for a vain-glorious exchange of catwalk behaviour, our guardians of the law sauntered off to find a bigger window to gaze into.

We went on shore and headed for the nearest Avis Renta car shop. We soon found it at the end of the harbour wall. A pretty young woman, in hire shop uniform of a blue and white spotted blouse and tight navy pencil skirt, sorted us out with a top-of-the- range BMW. We signed the papers, paid the huge sum in euros, and took possession of the gleaming silver thing that nestled in a yard behind the harbour wall. Luxurious leather seats and a smell of newness greeted us as I slipped behind the wheel. Gently easing the car out of the parking we drove down to our berth on the quay. I backed up with the boot facing the Mary Swift and we started to transfer our loot. First in went the 20 kg of gold bars in their 10kg metal cases. Two of those. Then the currency notes which were much bulkier and half filled the cavernous boot, followed by our own personal luggage and weaponry. Lastly we stashed the diamonds, but they were such a small package that they took up hardly any space. I jammed them down behind the spare wheel cover. By the time we'd finished the boot looked as normal as a filled boot would look if the occupants of the car were on their summer hols. Good. Ready for the drive across the mountains to Berne. We stashed a Kalashnikov and two hand guns in the front of the BMW, as previous experience had warned us better to be prepared than not. Locking the Mary Swift, and reporting to the harbourmasters office that we would be gone for a fortnight at least, we drove the gleaming silver monster out of Trieste harbour and set off along the northern coastal road towards Venice.

Italian drivers leave a lot to be desired in their attitudes to safety and politeness and after the first two or three incidents of hair-raising overtaking and just sheer silly speeding, I realised I needed to concentrate hugely on the driving. No chance then to admire the many shrines both amateur and professional that dotted the roadside where much-loved Giuseppe or Marco had met his maker whilst behind the wheel of the swift little Fiat or Seat that was to become their downfall.

The road took us round the Gulf of Venice and toward Verona. By late afternoon we were entering the environs of the great city of Milan. What a mistake. We should have bypassed it somehow. Any how, instead, like lambs to the slaughter, we drove unawares into the grasping, carbon monoxide, odious atmosphere of north Italy's premier city. The northern ring road, six lanes wide but unmarked, with huge plane trees edging it, was prey to the Lambrettas and buzz bomb scooters, ridden by fourteen-year-old kamikaze pilots with no helmets and a blithe disregard to the laws and rules of the road. Overlying the stink of exhaust, the blaring of car horns, the occasional louder lorry horn bellowed its discontent. We tried like mad to ease our way out of this hell, but it was at least two hours later that we eventually found our way onto the route through the Alps. Traffic quietened down as we climbed away from the plains and up into the mountains. We even started to enjoy the journey. The rocky crags that make up the foothills seemed to press into the roadside, giving the impression that the road was a lot narrower than it is. Then after some serious climbing, the ground suddenly opened up beside us and the whole vista of an alpine view fell into place beside us: a deep valley, green wooded, with a silver onward-rushing stream in the bottom, several hundred feet below us. The tarmacked road wound its way forward into an impressive double-fronted stone tunnel. The St Gotthard pass tunnel. Two road tunnels built side by side, one never used, but there should volume of traffic demand it in the future. The tunnel runs under the Alps for ten and a half miles, and a few years back an accident involving a lorry had a devastating effect with several travellers incinerated in the fire that followed and the cloying suffocating fumes generated. So many vehicles use the tunnel on a daily basis that there are often standstill-traffic jams within it. I wondered what that was like, as we pulled the beemer into the entrance of the tunnel. Overhead lights lit it as bright as day, and by the time we were well into the tunnel it seemed as if we'd never been anywhere else. Then we were out the other side and speeding through the border checkpoint where several bored-looking customs officials clocked us as we drove past. Switzerland and Italy are members of the Scvengen agreement, so no tedious border controls. The road stretched endlessly into the distance, and being the major route north it was a high quality structure and our modern car ate up the miles. We stopped at Bellinzola for a meal. Nothing much: just an omelette with wild mushrooms and a lovely green salad. Then it was on again, climbing higher into the Alps. The scenery was becoming more picturesque by the mile, and the spiky peaks of the Alps towered above us. As the evening gloaming started to set in, we arrived at Andermatt; a picturesque mountain-tourist town renowned for its skiing but just as well-known for its walking and the quality of the air. We pulled into the car park of the Gast Huss Muller and registered at reception.

'Yes sir, Madame, there is a double room available. Hans will carry your baggage.'

A youth in lederhosen, with the most well-defined thigh muscles ever seen on anyone not an athlete, carried our bags upwards to a lovely warm, wood-clad room with a balcony and a window overlooking the town. A few Swiss francs as a tip kept him and his thighs satisfied, and we went back down to explore the town. It is a lovely place in the full meaning of the Swiss word. Everything neatly in its place, and a place for everything. I suddenly had a memory of my friend Al, who as a hippy on his way home from Greece in the Sixties, was refused entry into Switzerland. The official reason: too much like a vagrant and might frighten the locals. Turned back, he had to detour through Italy and France. Pissed him off no end and he never forgave the Swiss!

Anyway, we weren't hippies, even though our philosophy might have been. We were wealthy, very wealthy, tourists with expensive wristwatches. So there! We called into a bar and had a beer. Sitting at a table outside with a cold Stella frothing in a long glass in front of me, I was annoyed when a slim dark haired middle-European type of a man slipped into the chair opposite.

'I want no trouble,' he said.

What now, I thought. So much terror had come our way over the last few months, what new thing might this be? He showed me the muzzle of a small handgun, which he kept pointed at Catriona's stomach.

'! want all the currency notes you are carrying in your car. You go and fetch them here in a bag, whilst I entertain your companion.' He grinned; just like Al Arabi would have, with a predatory shark's mouthful of teeth.

'You have half an hour.' He glanced at his watch. 'Be back here by seven at the latest or she dies.'

He meant it, I could tell, so I scurried off in the direction of the beemer; thoughts of how to retain our stash flowing round my head, but always coming up with a blank. When I reached the car, it was a good ten minutes work to transfer the cash into a green plastic sack that happened to be lying in the boot. I stuffed the sack full, but that left me with a largish stash of notes still in the boot. I slammed the lid and locked up. Throwing the plastic sac back over my shoulder, I hotfooted it back to the café. Mr Mid European and Catriona were sitting in a tense looking eyeball-to-eyeball stand off.

'Here's the money.' I hoicked the sack up onto the table. The green snake eyes swivelled towards it.

'Open it.'

I pulled the neck of the sack back to show him the neatly packaged currency notes. 'It's all there I hope'

'Of course. Now bugger off why don't you.'

He smiled his sickly smile and produced a mobile from a jacket pocket. Mumbling some foreign words into it, he sat back and waited. Within a few minutes a black-windowed Audi drove into the square. The back door swung open and our robber climbed in. With a squeal of rubber, the car left the square and disappeared who-knows-where into the depths of the town.

'I got his number at least' said Catriona, 'though I doubt I'll be able to access that on our police computer.'

'No, but we could report a theft to the police here and see what they came up with.' 'Yeah, or ask Angus for help! Better idea, lets get on that.'

We retired to our room in the Gast Haus Muller and Catriona put a call through to Angus on the satellite phone. After a few bleeps and whirrs his voice came through clear as a bell.

'Well what can I do for you heroes, and did you know Gaddafi is dead! Killed in Sirte whilst hiding in a drain!'

We shook our heads in amazement. Did this mean the fighting in Libya was over? More questions than answers thrown up by this new info. We asked after the number plate on the black Audi, and in due course Angus came back with the answer. Registered to a Croatian betting syndicate, known for their connections to organised crime. What's more, a registered office address was given for the betting arm of their operations, in Berne of all places. Catriona and I discussed it and decided to visit the offices and get our money back, or failing that we'd torch the place. That'd teach 'em for having the effrontery to steal twice-nicked money from people not entitled to it! Dirty money engenders dirty thoughts, and I thought back in wistful dismay to the halcyon days of innocence before all this toxic shit had gone down, and how it had changed us. I asked Catriona how she felt, and it was a mirror image of my own feelings. We crawled into bed and upon the comfy mattresses of the guesthouse,with the warm duvets over us, fell asleep

After a breakfast of stunning simplicity, and having settled up the bill, we were on the road in the direction of Berne by nine-thirty. Not much traffic apart from the ubiquitous trucks of the EC rumbling through the Alps, and by midday we could see the multi church spires of

Berne ahead of us. I'd heard a story about a flat dweller in Berne who wanted a piano winched up into his top floor flat. Everything had gone well until the unhitching of the shackles. At that point, the fat Swiss lad ostensibly handling the top end of the operation, undid the wrong shackle, causing the whole ensemble to fall four stories on to the cobbles below. Luckily, no one was hurt, the piano was matchwood however and the good burgers of Berne enacted an ordinance forbidding pianos on any floor but the ground. The other interesting fact about Berne is its bear-baiting pit. Situated on the edge of town, it dates back hundreds of years and consists of a fifteen to twenty-foot deep stone-lined, open topped chamber about twenty feet across, into which the poor brown creatures were placed and bets taken on the outcome of the baiting against dogs. It must have been popular, for Berne's official logo is of a bear tethered to a ragged staff. We drove past this monument and on into the centre of town. We parked in a side street off Victoria Platz and locked the car. Our destination was in Heissingerstrasse, a seedy little cobbled alley that ran back towards Victoria platz. We walked slowly down this alleyway until we came to number 20. A brass sign on the wall next to the door proclaimed it as The Centre For Croatian Peace Studies. I gave a hollow laugh as I tried the door. Surprise, surprise, it opened! We slipped into a tall baroque hall with an art nouveau wrought-iron staircase winding upwards to the first floor, and highly polished quarry tiles of an early 20th century design on the floor. No one about. We tiptoed to the staircase and started up. On the first floor there were four rooms, each with a substantial door fronting them. Nothing to say what was behind each door, so we started to try each one. The first on the left opened to reveal a committee room or boardroom with a substantial oval walnut dining table around which were several dining chairs. The next room was a kitchen, and the third room: bingo. An office with computers, filing cabinets, and all the accoutrements of a modern office. Catriona placed me on watch by the door, and settled down in front of the first screen and powered it up. I could hear the sound of the computer keyboard as she hacked into their secrets, and still no one appeared. This was most peculiar. What organisation kept all its records open to anyone who cared to break in! I felt a bit intimidated, and eased the plastic Glock hand gun out of my jacket pocket. Better safe than sorry I thought.

Catriona called through to me. 'All done, let's get out of here!'

I wanted to check out the fourth room and duly did so. There was a large old-fashioned three lever Swiss-made safe within, and wonders of wonders on the floor beside it a very familiar looking green plastic bag. I peered inside and, yes, it was our money, or Gaddafi's money, or the Libyan people's money. Whosoever could lay claim to it, I was having it, and scooping up the bag I backed out of the room. Catriona was waiting impatiently at the top of the stairs and we left the building the way we'd come in.

Back in the car I asked her what she'd done to their computers.

'Oh nothing much. I inserted a small programme that would activate any time anyone laid a bet of over one-hundred euros; twenty percent of the bet and of any winnings will now go straight to the Save The Children Fund in Zurich! I hugged her tight causing her to nearly lose control of the car, but she's a better driver than I by a long shot. We drove sedately to another tree-lined avenue in the suburbs away from the hustle and bustle of the commercial shopping heart of the town and located the two banks where we had appointments.

Clutching the bag of diamonds that was the pay-off to the killer of Yvonne Fletcher and was ostensibly our reason for being here, I went into the hallowed portals of the bank. A bald headed Swiss clerk in a morning coat bustled up to me and said something in Swiss. I replied that I had an appointment and his demeanour changed rapidly and he lead me through into the back offices. There I was placed under strict scrutiny, having my fingerprints taken, my passport examined in minute detail and my MI6 story gone over twice. Eventually when the officials in the room were satisfied as to my bona fides, they gratefully relieved me of the diamonds and gave me a very small paper receipt for the goods. Then with no more than a perfunctory goodbye, they ushered me off the premises.

So much for the much vaunted Swiss politeness and desire to do business. Maybe they had too many customers and a scruffy-looking Scotsman was not one they relished having.

Back to the car and down the next tree-lined street and into the Belossi Bank Spittalglass. Now this was a different kettle of fish I must say. Behind a glass and chrome façade, modern-looking Swiss people came and went with a purpose that boded well for our money. We parked in the secure-looking car park, locked the car and went in. A charming young woman with her hair tied back in a chignon came over straight away and ushered us into a back office.

'We would like to deposit some assets in your bank,' Catriona said.

The young woman nodded. 'How much would that be?'

'One million Stirling in currency notes, Seven-hundred and fifty-thousand pounds worth in gold bullion bars, and approximately two million sterling in diamonds both cut and uncut.'

The smooth Swiss woman hardly blinked. Maybe this sort of transaction was commonplace. She asked some delicate question about ownership of the assets, but nothing was written down, after we had given our specimen signatures, read the conditions of the Swiss bankers and been allocated a safe deposit box. Within five minutes two gleaming new plastic debit cards with our details on them were handed over, and she summoned two burly guards who came with us to the car and carried in our money. Half an hour later, and three and three quarter million pounds wealthier, we left the bank like a couple of Swiss cats who'd just got at the double cream. Outside I high-fived the girl I loved, and gave her a smacking great kiss which was warmly returned. We climbed into the car and drove away from the bank.

We stopped at a patisserie for coffee and sacher torte and discussed our next moves.

'I think it's too dangerous to drive back to the Mary Swift. The Croatians may well be looking out for us, also it's too far to drive across Germany. I think we should fly home. We'll be there by tomorrow, and we could afford first class!'

Catriona's face lit up. 'What a brilliant idea. I'll call Angus and he can send someone to meet us at Glasgow airport.'

Bern airport proved to be a winner with flight availability to London City airport and then on to Glasgow. Business class the best upgrade for us, and by four-thirty that afternoon we watched from our seats as the plane thundered into the sky and onwards north towards the skies of the UK.

Our connection at London City, smooth as a vicar's forehead, and our onward destination, Glasgow, gleaming like diamonds in the gloaming as we circled the airfield, before putting down smoothly on home soil.

A man in a gabardine mac, belted in severely and with a suspicious looking bulge under the armpit, like something out of an Ealing spy film, greeted us at customs. 'Davie Baxter? Catriona Maxwell?' We nodded. 'Follow me please.'

He ushered us through the arrival lounge and out into the concourse where stood a black Range Rover.

'Climb in, we're going to MI6 HQ.'

Dutifully we did as he asked and he whisked us through the streets of Glasgow to yet another secluded tree-lined avenue not dissimilar from those of the Bern Banking sector. The car pulled up at a substantial late Victorian mansion. The twin, double oak doors fast-barred against any entry. Our guide swiped an entry card through a reader and the door opened. Inside a hum of activity greeted us. Purposeful-looking young people not more than in their mid twenties, came and went in a flurry of activity, and then there in front of us was that unreconstructed hippie Angus, grinning from ear to ear. He embraced Catriona and gave her two kisses on her cheeks. He shook my hand almost off my wrist and ushered us both into a back room. A double Bushmills apiece and settled in three club chairs, he proceeded to debrief us. After an hour of intensive conversation; some very searching questions about various fire fights and interventions along the way, Angus sat back in his chair and said, 'Well you two. HM government thanks you most sincerely for all your help, and although you are amongst the unsung and unpaid heroes, your contribution has not gone unnoticed. I would expect a gong sometime in the New Year.'

I snorted, and brought out the dinner gong joke.

He laughed and said, 'No, it'd be more in the order of the Victorian Order of Gallantry.'

Suitably crushed I sank back into the club chair.

'And now the pair of you are due some leave. I expect you'll want to visit the House in the Woods. Give me a bell in a couple of weeks. I think I'll have another job for you !.......

The End